BROKEN IN THE BACK BAY

Sarah E. Stewart

Copyright © 2015 Sarah E Stewart
All rights reserved.

ISBN-13: 9781511714136
ISBN-10: 1511714131

To my husband, Brian, for his endless love, support, belief, strength, and encouragement.
To Sarah Judd McGuiness and Diana Clark for their years of tireless faith and confidence.
To my family and friends who have been pillars of support throughout my life.

TABLE OF CONTENTS

Preface	vii
Eva	1
Lauren	3
Shelly	5
Brioche Technologies Home Office	9
Lauren	11
Eva	14
Jackie	16
Lauren	29
Eva	34
Shelly	38
Eva	40
Lauren	43
Jackie	46
Shelly	53
Eva, Christmas Day	55
Shelly	57
Session 1	61
Brioche Technologies Home Office	66
Session 2	68
Katz's Apartment	73
Session 3	75
Jackie	88
Shelly	90
Eva	92
Jackie	94
Session 4	99
Eva	105
Jackie	111
Shelly	113

Jackie, Saturday Morning	114
Lauren	116
Eva, Sunday Morning Pickup	118
Lauren	123
Brioche Technologies Home Office	125
Session 5	127
Eva	134
Tony's Office	135
Lauren	137
Shelly	139
Eva	143
Shelly	146
Brioche Technologies Home Office	154
Saturday Morning Makeup Session	156
Jackie	166
Lauren	170
Shelly	173
Tony's Office	178
Eva	180
Jackie	184
Tony, Sunday Morning, 8:00 A.M.	185
Eva	196
Eva, Monday Night	198
Tuesday Morning	204
Epilogue	207
Questions for Discussion	210

PREFACE

If you had six months to live, what would you do? If you have lived your six months, what do you regret?

EVA

Eva has been artfully nodding as the therapist presents all of the rules of confidentiality. Eva knows the therapy game; she knows all about confidentiality and HIPAA. Eva smiled at the appropriate times and gave her verbal agreement when needed, all the while sizing up the woman sitting in front of her based on the office and its contents. The books that sit on the shelves are eclectic and elementary; Eva has read them all. The diplomas displayed on the walls are all from state universities; they are no match for Eva's inherent intellect, let alone her Ivy League education. The furniture is cheap and tired. Eva estimates that she probably makes fifteen to twenty times more annually than the therapist. Yes, they live in very different worlds. Before the therapist can even ask one question about why Eva was there, Eva knows she is not going to be good enough. Eva is already angry with herself for taking precious time out of her busy life and bothering to make this appointment. How could anyone who comes to this same office day in and day out even begin to relate to Eva's frustrations and concerns, let alone her life?

"Pardon me?" Eva is not quite sure she heard the therapist correctly.

"I said, if you leave, that's fine, but you will still have to pay for the session, as you already agreed to the cancellation policy when you made the appointment online."

"Who said anything about leaving?" Eva responds firmly.

Jackie simply points with an open hand toward Eva. Eva takes a look down at herself and sees that she is on the edge of her seat with both feet on the ground and her purse strap wrapped around her hand. Eva is clearly in the position of someone about to walk out the door, not someone who is about to sit through a fifty-minute therapy session. Eva smiles. She unwraps her hand from her purse, sits back in her chair, and decides to stay for at least this session. Eva appreciates Jackie's quick assessment, her business acumen, and, most importantly, her confidence.

Jackie is relieved to see Eva's exit stance dissipate. She could tell by Eva's half-completed self-assessment that if she even showed up today, Eva was going to be a challenge. And so far, after all of five minutes, Eva is living up to Jackie's expectations.

"So, Eva, before we really begin today, I read what you completed of your self-assessment."

Eva nods. She has been waiting patiently for the standard question on why she did not complete the assessment and the long-winded explanation on how valuable the self-assessment tool is for a new therapeutic relationship.

"As a therapist, I have to get some clarification on one question. With regard to ever feeling suicidal or having any suicidal ideation, you wrote that you do not have acute suicidal thoughts but are passively suicidal. Would you elaborate for me?"

Eva smiles. "Jackie, I am an Ivy League–educated woman in her forties who works eighty-plus hours per week, has at least one drink per day, and smokes. Some would call my habits avoidance; some would call my habits addictions. They may not kill me today, but I am well aware that one of those things or the combination of those things will eventually kill me. So, yes, I would say I am passively suicidal."

LAUREN

"Oh my God!" Lauren can't believe her eyes as she enters the hotel suite. It is the most beautiful thing she had ever seen. It was like she had walked into a palace. She turns to Greg, who stands tall and looks devastatingly handsome in the entryway. "Are you kidding me?"

Greg smiles brightly as Lauren walks through the living room toward the wall of floor-to-ceiling windows that give the most impressive view of the ocean. She turns to her right and sees double doors opening to the grand bedroom. She looks at Greg and squeals with excitement. She walks into the bedroom; to her right is an inviting king-size bed that faces the ocean. The bathroom is straight ahead and is better than any spa she has ever been in. The soaking tub is lined with new white candles and sits parallel to more floor-to-ceiling windows facing the ocean. Lauren squeals again. She races back through the bedroom into the living area and looks toward the door. Greg is not there. She looked out toward the ocean, and Greg is standing on the massive deck, smiling back at her. He motions toward the table on his left. Lauren's eyes follow his hand.

"Oh, my God," Lauren whispers as she covers her mouth. On the table is the most tremendous display of fruit, cheese, chocolate, flowers, and a bottle of Dom with two glasses. As Lauren walks out onto the balcony, she is hit with the warm Bahamian breeze that wraps around her body and seemingly squeezes out all of her stress. She stands for a moment and takes another deep breath. She looks at Greg and says, "Thank you. This is fucking amazing." She walks up to him and wraps her arms around him. "Scratch that—*you* are fucking amazing!"

SHELLY

"You know what I wish…I wish there was a little bomb on Facebook. Instead of just the choice of ignoring or "liking" things, there was a bomb, with a mean, ugly face on it; and when we don't like what someone says, we could ugly face bomb it. You know, instead of just ignoring it, we could literally, at the click of a button, ugly face bomb…'Yeah, you suck.' Seriously, why just the feel-good stuff. I mean, sure, it's great and easy to say we like something, so why can't I just as easily say…not so much. OK, maybe not so aggressive with the ugly face bomb, but why not thumbs down? Wouldn't that stop people from constantly posting bullshit? My life is great; here are me and all my friends, without you. Here is me and my happy family, here is me and my great partner, here are my great kids. See how great everything is in my life? It is like high school for the midlifers. It sucks."

Jackie is always amused by Shelly's little rants. "Did something specific happen on Facebook?"

"It's not specific, no. It's every single day in my world, both work and life. People are constantly posting pictures of themselves with this group or that group. It's like, 'How cool am I in our world? Not only was I hanging out with the cool kids, all of the other cool kids who were not with us have commented and "liked" it.' I work in this world that is supposed to be so focused on helping people, but the only thing they are focused on is themselves. It is the most narcissistic, crazy-ass thing. Seriously, they just hang out with each other and post constantly about spending time with each other. If you are all so busy hanging out with each other, who the fuck are you helping? I mean, really, you are a therapist, Jackie; you help people all day long. Are all of your Facebook posts pictures of you hanging out with other therapists? Do you have like a top-twenty-therapists-in-Boston group, who everyone wants to be like, and you all just hang out together and post on Facebook all day long?"

"No."

"Exactly." Shelly continues after her therapist gives her the only obvious answer. "You and all the other therapists are actually busy doing your jobs, helping people. I don't know what the hell my job is. I thought it was about helping people. But now, these people in my field, who are the supposed best, are just hanging out together all the time posting pictures, together, at all the big events. When do they work? When do they do the stuff that needs to be done, if all they are doing is meeting with each other?"

"But aren't you one of the cool kids? One of the ones everyone wants to be like? And aren't people coming after you now?" Jackie is still uncertain as to what is truly bothering Shelly.

"Yes, but I do not want any of it. I want to leave all of it behind. I want nothing to do with an industry that is so self-centered and so self-serving. It breaks my heart. I hate how much money they make off of other people's pain. I hate it!" Shelly lets out a big sigh. It felt good to get that off her chest. She had been fuming all day yesterday, but she knew she would be meeting with her therapist, so she decided to hold onto her anger until she got right here.

"Well, technically, lots of people make money off of others' pain, including myself," says Jackie. She is still trying to untangle Shelly's anger.

"It's more than that, Jackie. It is exclusive. Not inclusive. It is not transparent. It is quite sick."

"Are we still talking about your disdain for Facebook?"

"It's all of it. Yes, Facebook triggers me, but I want out of my industry."

And there it is, Jackie thinks to herself, *right back to Shelly's unhappiness with her work.* "OK, so smaller issue and larger issue. Which one do you want to tackle first?"

"I know—Facebook. I should just not go on it, but I feel like I have to. All I hear all the time is, 'Oh yeah, I saw that on Facebook.' Or, 'Did you see this on Facebook? Did you get my invitation on Facebook?' It is like if I ignore it or go off Facebook, I somehow miss everything that I am clearly already missing. It is this vicious cycle. I hate it. It makes me so angry and depressed, I want to just hurl my phone off the Mass Ave Bridge, but then I would have to jump in after it. Maybe that's not a bad idea."

"Which part?"

"Both."

"Do you want to kill yourself?" Jackie hates having to address the obvious fact that Shelly is just being sarcastic. But anytime her clients say things like that, she has to check it out.

"Some days," says Shelly. "But no, not really."

"Are you sure?"

"Yes, Jackie, I am sure. I am not suicidal." Shelly is a bit annoyed that Jackie even thinks that she would ever kill herself. Although she has to be honest—the thought has crossed her mind more than once. She would never actually do it; she just sometimes thinks of it when she is overwhelmed. It is just a fleeting thought. She needs a vacation from her life, not a permanent exit from it.

"OK, well good, because, you know, that is a whole thing in my world that we take quite seriously. I would have to keep you here, call 911, and send you to the ER. Then I would go to the ER and try and have you committed for seventy-two hours to be sure you were safe. So, with that said, can you look me in the eye and tell me that you are safe and not suicidal, and that if you feel unsafe or suicidal, you will reach out to me or 911?"

"What? Yes, Jackie; I am not suicidal."

"OK, good, but if you feel it at all, you will reach out to me or 911."

"Yes, on Facebook." Shelly smiles at her own sarcastic wit.

"Perfect," says Jackie. "Now, of course, we could spend some time discussing ways to limit your time on Facebook. However, I feel that would serve as a distraction from the bigger issue that you have been stuck with for quite some time."

"Yes," says Shelly. "My job, I know. I go round and round. I hate it, Jackie, and my disdain for it is getting stronger."

"Yes, it appears to be."

"But Jackie, I can't just leave it. I mean, Boston is very expensive to live in. I need this job."

Jackie could have said Shelly's comment for her. This battle with her job, the love of the money but the disdain for the work and the industry, has been going on for a long time. Jackie feels as stuck with trying to help Shelly move forward as Shelly does in her job. Jackie knows that now is as good of a time as any to try and move Shelly through this struggle.

"Shelly, we have been circling over this for quite some time. I have an idea, if you would be open to it."

Shelly sits back in her chair and gives Jackie a positive nod to proceed.

BRIOCHE TECHNOLOGIES HOME OFFICE

"Mark, calm down; the stock will come back up. It just took a dive based on the speculations, and I repeat speculations, that we will not get approval on our latest drug. They do not know what they're talking about. I am the man sitting in the room with the board, the physicians, and the chemists. I am the one who knows what is going on with the FDA, and I am the one who knows it is going to get approved."

"One million dollars is a lot of money, John. I have a right to be concerned."

"Mark, I am telling you. We have been friends for over forty years. Our friendship is why I brought this opportunity to you. You will be rich beyond your wildest dreams. It is getting approved. I guarantee it. Trust me, end of January. Relax and enjoy the holiday season."

John hangs up the phone, feeling confident he has just bought himself more time—but not much more time. His office phone rings, and he looks and sees it is his assistant. He inhales quickly; he needs to maintain his cool.

"Yes, Stella," he says.

"Mr. Katz is on the line for you, sir."

"Put him through; thank you, Stella." After a moment, he says, "Katz, what can I do for you?"

"Hi, John. I just wanted to know how the call went with Mark."

"Fine. I think I bought us some more time. How did things go with the Chicago investors?"

"They are nervous, John, but they calmed down after the presentation and a good deal of wine. I will need to visit them again soon. How much time do we have?"

"Six weeks, Katz. Eight weeks tops. I hope you have your affairs in order."

"Ha! I will see you after the holidays, John. Enjoy."

John hangs up the phone and calls his assistant. "Stella, I need Eva's social for her bonus check. Will you get that for me? She is not answering her phone."

"Yes, sir, I will get it for you right away."

LAUREN

"Well, in all honesty, I don't have time for a relationship," Lauren is saying. "I am so busy. My business has exploded this year, and I am very grateful for that. Completely exhausted, but grateful."

"Congratulations on your achievements," says Jackie. "They are impressive."

"Thank you. And I am growing the business. As it stands, I plan to bump Maria up to a full-time consultant and bring someone new onboard in the assistant role. It is really exciting. I work most weekends. I truly do not know how to work in a relationship. I date, but it is the same cycle, you know. When the 'wedding season' goes in to full swing, I do not have any weekends free, and that is typically the spring through the fall. People want dates on the weekends; they want to go away on the weekends; they want to do things with their partner on the weekends; and I just can't. So I guess I am not an appealing partner for many guys."

"Well, some of this is about priorities, and some of it is about what you truly want."

"My priority is my business."

"And what do you want?" asks Jackie.

Lauren pauses to think about her response. She knows what she wants; she's just not sure why she is having a hard time verbalizing it.

If you are going to say it out loud to anyone, your therapist is a good start. Lauren begins to speak but then hesitates for a second longer before saying, "I want both, actually. Does that make me sound greedy?"

And there it is, Jackie thinks to herself. "Greedy? How so?"

"Well, you know, I mean..." Lauren has to pause and catch her breath. She is feeling anxious at the question, like there is only one right answer. She has to answer the question correctly; she does not want her therapist to think she is stupid. Lauren sits up straight and moves to the edge of the couch. "I mean, I do not want to be looked at like 'Who does she think she is? She has a great business, a great man.' I don't want people to judge me or be envious of me."

"Is that your fear?" asks Jackie.

"Yes; I mean, I have a lot of fears, but I am a people pleaser, Jackie. I want...I *need* people to like me; so yes, that is a big fear."

"So, the obstacle to you having or continuing to have a very successful business and a relationship is that people may judge you and not like you?"

"Well, no, it is not an obstacle, but I would not want that to happen," says Lauren.

"Lauren, when you first came to see me three months ago, you were rather upset about a recent breakup."

"Not just a breakup, Jackie—a complete disappearance. We went on an amazing trip to the Bahamas. I mean the trip was quite spectacular, the suite we had was incredible, he paid for everything; I felt like a princess. He told me he was in love with me. When we returned home," Lauren paused for a second. She got weird feeling a very uncomfortable bad feeling.

Jackie observes Lauren as she pauses in her story. The look in Lauren's eyes becomes very distant as if she is remembering something. Jackie waits and then finally says, "Lauren?"

Lauren startles from her trance. "Yes. I'm sorry. I just remembered something for work. I have to book a honeymoon sutie. Sorry, occupational hazard. Where was I?"

"You were telling me what happened when you go home from the Bahamas."

"Yes. Well, we returned home and he disappeared. He just removed himself from my life. He just went away without any reason. Maybe he had a reason, but I wouldn't know, because he never called, e-mailed, texted, nothing. I am in my forties, Jackie, not twenty-two." Lauren corrects Jackie immediately so as to keep the record straight. A breakup she could handle; sixty miles per hour to zero was a different story.

"Yes, Lauren; my apologies. It was the quick, unexplained exit that would leave most in a rather somber and in a frustrated state." Jackie pauses to be certain she had restated Lauren's reasons for seeking counseling in an acceptable manner.

Lauren nods in agreement.

Jackie continues, "After having experienced something so drastic, what are some of the obstacles? And I don't mean logistical obstacles; those we can remove and get around. What are some of your internal obstacles?"

Lauren sits back against the couch. She stares at the floor and shakes her head. She starts to speak before looking up. "I don't know." Lauren looks up at Jackie, composes herself, and continues, "I've had plenty of breakups, Jackie; and yes, that one was hard, and I hated not knowing why he just went away. But I am not sure what my internal obstacles are."

Jackie feels like banging her head against the wall. She wishes Lauren would just admit her fear out loud so they could move forward. She has to push Lauren, but not too hard. Jackie knows she has to maintain a delicate balance with Lauren for fear of triggering her. Jackie is even more cautious after seeing the blank look on Lauren's face as she discussed her trip to the Bahamas. She can't push Lauren too hard, but it is obvious to Jackie there is a lot more going on with Lauren than what she is actually presenting. "Lauren, I have an out-of-the-box idea; would you be open to hearing it?"

EVA

Bang. The incredibly loud noise jolts Eva out of bed and onto her feet. She stops for a second and listens. Her heart is pounding against her chest. *Bang.* She hears the noise again, hangs her head, and lets out a big sigh of relief. She fumbles for the switch on the lamp on the bedside table. She sits down on the bed, looks up, and takes a deep breath. Her heart is still pounding in her chest. She looks around the hotel room, refamiliarizing herself with her surroundings. The bangs were just hotel doors slamming. "You are OK," she says to herself. As she begins to calm down, she notices that the sheet under her hand is wet, very wet. She puts her hand on her T-shirt and finds that it is soaked. "Shit, another nightmare," Eva whispers to herself. She tries to remember: she remembers feeling scared, but she thought it was from the loud noise startling her awake. Maybe that is not what woke her up. Eva walks over to her suitcase and pulls out a clean T-shirt, slips it on, and throws the wet one in the plastic bag with her dirty clothes. She walks around the king-sized bed and slips under the covers on the dry side of the bed. She lies in bed, staring at the ceiling, and begins to remember. She closes her eyes and prays, "Please God, please just make it stop." As the fearful memories start to fill her mind, she grabs the television remote, turns on the TV, and begins to flip through the channels.

She reassures herself that staying awake is the better than the alternative—the risk of another nightmare. She props herself up with pillows and stares blankly at the screen, never bothering to wipe away the tears that begin streaming down her face.

JACKIE

Jackie walks into her supervisor's office on a snowy Friday afternoon. Her mind is racing as she begins to take off all winter layers. Jackie sometimes calls Janice her therapist, but Janice is really someone Jackie pays to provide her with supervision. Jackie has a small yet successful private practice in Boston, Massachusetts. She lives in Boston's South End neighborhood but keeps a practice in the Beacon Hill area. Everyone likes to try to tell her she should open an office in the South End, where the rent is cheaper and she would have a shorter commute. But Boston is a small city, and Jackie likes to have a bit of separation between her work life and her home life; even if it's only twenty blocks, she rarely goes out in Beacon Hill, so having her office in Beacon Hill is just peace of mind. And really, how can walking twenty blocks even be considered a commute?

Every morning and every evening, Jackie can take a myriad of routes to and from work. Her favorite these days is taking Dartmouth Street to Newbury Street, walking up Newbury Street (one of the most famous shopping streets in the country) and admiring all of the window displays along the way. At the end of Newbury, she crosses Arlington Street and walks through the Boston Public Garden, which, even in the dead of winter, is still a sight to see. She then takes a left on Charles Street and a right onto Beacon Street. This puts her at the base of Beacon Hill—which is exactly what it is, the big hill on Beacon Street that takes you right up to the statehouse. On one side of Beacon Street is the Boston Common, and on the other are the quaint little Beacon Hill streets that are a mix of commercial buildings and beautiful brownstones, some of which are actually owned in their entirety as a single residence! In the morning hours, Beacon Street is usually bustling with exercisers, government workers, and other professionals, who are typically making their way over the hill into the financial district. However, if one were to just wait until about 10:00 a.m., the street would still have its fair share of professionals and exercisers, but it would also be filled with tourists and small groups (often students) led by a professional tour guide explaining all about Boston's rich history.

Jackie's practice consists of what most in the profession would call "the worried well." She would tend to agree. She is a good therapist. Her practice is private pay, and she has a waiting list. But the work she does now is nothing like the work she did for the first ten years of her career. In the beginning, she worked in a locked psychiatric hospital with adolescents and young adults. It was brutal, and she loved every minute of it. At the time, at twenty-five years of age, she thought she would never want to work with any other population besides adolescents and their families. The kids had so much energy, they kept her on her toes, and the families were complicated; the work was challenging. But year after year of having to sit in a room and tell a mom and dad that their beloved Yale-attending son just had his first schizophrenic break or that their daughter was in the emergency room because of a heroin overdose took its toll on Jackie. After ten years of working in that highly charged, emotionally and mentally taxing atmosphere, Jackie decided to leave and go into private practice.

Initially she did begin working with adolescents, but as time went on, the parents started to refer friends and relatives, and her practice morphed into what it is today. She primarily works with adults in their late twenties to early fifties, with some couples thrown in the mix. She is often surprised at how much she enjoys working with this population; yet, she is equally aware of how she herself, at forty-three, can sometimes relate all too well to the issues her clients present. Hence, this brings us back to the moment, as she is waiting for her supervisor.

Janice comes out to greet Jackie promptly at 6:00 p.m., the scheduled time of their session. They hug, as they are friends, not just colleagues. Janice stands about five foot two and barley weighs one hundred pounds. Her slight build is no indication of her clinical savvy and directness. Her face at times looks stern and sharp, but she is an amazing clinician and has such a warm heart. Again, her exterior presence poorly represents her interior. Jackie and Janice meet once a month for an hour; however, when Jackie has a difficult caseload, and their schedules allow, they increase the meetings to twice a month. Thankfully, this month, even with the craziness of the holidays, their schedules were able to accommodate a second session, because Jackie needs it.

They head back into Janice's office, chatting about the miserable Boston weather, both of them looking forward to spring not only for their own sakes but also for the sake of their clients' mental health. There are certain things one learns as therapist. The things once often thought of as myths are sometimes very real. Two of those are that the weather can greatly affect people's moods and that there really is some truth to the full moon bringing out all the "crazy" in people. Jackie plops herself down in the corner of Janice's large brown leather sofa. Janice's office is inviting yet professional.

"Well, my dear," Janice begins, "I know the last time we met, you were struggling with some of your clients and some of the issues they were bringing up for you. So, where are you today?"

"I feel as though we have a good handle on what issues were being brought up for me and what signals I needed to pay attention to and stay on top of. Where I am today is rather stuck with those same three clients. I have a potential idea, and I wanted to bounce it off of you."

Jackie proceeds to review her three clients with Janice and says that over the last two weeks, she has asked each of her clients to begin group work and that they have all agreed. The group is set to begin in two weeks, right after the New Year. Jackie has asked them all to prepare a brief synopsis of the main issue they are each presenting in therapy, which will then be presented to the group.

"My biggest concern at this point, Janice, is starting the group and getting the three women to bond enough to lessen the superficial nature of each of their presentations."

Janice looks at Jackie with the questioning motherly look that she has mastered so well. "Really, the initial bonding process? That is your biggest concern?"

"Well, it is my most pressing concern right now," says Jackie. "Why? Do you think there is something I should be more worried about?"

"I do. But first Jackie, let us address your primary concern. And I will begin by pointing out your language, your 'most pressing concern.' Jackie, your language should be a warning sign to you. You know you cannot force or control the process, especially in a group. I understand why this is a concern to you, especially considering this is a six-week group. However, I need to point out to you to really keep yourself in check when it comes to forcing or trying to control the process. When one of your patients is stuck, this is your biggest weakness. Now you are embarking on a group process in which three of your patients are stuck. I think this group is a great idea, and personally, I would love to be there and watch it unfold. However, your first priority should be keeping yourself in check and letting the process happen."

"You are absolutely right, Janice. I am feeling the pressure, and I am going right into my control mode. I will have to be hyperaware of that. Now, before I ask the bigger question of you, do you have any thoughts about a good way to start the group?"

"Jackie, no one I know is better at getting a group started than you. I've seen you do it clinically; I've seen you do it socially. You have the biggest bag of tricks and the incredible skill set to go with it. Again, you are having trouble because of the pressure you are putting on this process. Go with what you know will work in this setting, and let the process happen. As for your bigger question, control over the process is not the only thing you will have to be acutely aware of."

"I know. And I have thought a lot about that. I am well aware that I can overidentify with each of these women. Because of that, I was hoping we could, while I am facilitating this group, meet twice a month for the next few months. I think I will certainly need to keep myself balanced for their sake and mine."

"Agreed." Janice, nods her head with a half-smile, "Shall we schedule them all now?"

"Let's!" Jackie replies, laughing, knowing all too well how much she is going to need the supervision.

Jackie leaves Janice's office with five appointments scheduled over the next two and half months. It is now 7:15 p.m.; it is dark outside, as it has been for hours, and still snowing. Janice's office is, thankfully, just ten blocks from Jackie's house. She turns the corner from Commonwealth Avenue and heads up Dartmouth Street toward home. The snow is beautiful. It is coming down lightly, with barely any wind, which makes walking in the snow actually pleasant. There is something beautiful about the snow in the city. When it falls, the traffic lightens, people go home early, it is fresh and white, and the city becomes quieter, rather peaceful. You have to enjoy these moments, because tomorrow morning everything changes: you have to shovel, and the snow gets dirty and quickly becomes a hassle. However, on a Friday evening in December, with the city lit up with all of the holiday lights, it is just spectacular.

Jackie enjoys her ten-block trudge along the snowy sidewalks. Her mind is still racing. She knows Janice is right. She can find the right opening for the group to really break down some barriers in order to facilitate a more open process. However, these women who have agreed to try the group process could bring up issues for her. These are all issues she has dealt with; however, she still needs to be very careful of her boundaries. *We are all single women, about the same age, living in the same city. We are bound to have some similar issues*, Jackie thinks to herself.

Jackie reaches her street, which is one of the cutest in Boston. It is perfectly placed between the Back Bay and the South End. It is all brownstones, mostly condo conversions, and about 70 percent owner occupied. In a city full of renters, due to the high student population, this means that Jackie lives on a street that is slightly more age-appropriate. She unlocks the front door and enters the breezeway, grabs her mail, unlocks the second set of doors, and heads inside. Her brownstone consists of three units: the first floor is rented; the second floor is owned by her favorite couple, Tom and Rick; and Jackie is on the "penthouse" level, which actually consists of the third and fourth floors and one killer roof deck. She always feels like the luckiest woman when she comes home. Her place is spectacular. And she was fortunate enough, depending on how you look at it (home ownership does have its headaches), to be in the right place financially at exactly the right time.

She brushes off the snow as she heads up the stairs. OK, maybe she's not the luckiest woman; the luckiest would have an elevator. She passes by Tom and Rick's door, and out pops Rick.

"Sweetheart!" Rick roars while extending his arms. "Look at you, you little snowball. Did you get my text?"

Jackie leans in to give Rick a kiss on the cheek, not wanting to get him all wet from the snow. "No, love, I just walked home from Janice's office, so I haven't even looked at my phone."

"Well, you just run right upstairs and put on some comfy clothes. Tom and I have made dinner, and we have some fabulous wine. Oh, but not too comfy, Jackie; we have a friend coming over in thirty minutes—a straight friend. So primp up and be down here in fifteen so we can fill you in."

"Rick!" Jackie whines.

"What? No expectations—but he's super cute. Trust me. Go!"

Jackie turns to head up the last flight of stairs, and Rick stops her, "Actually Jackie, might I suggest those cute jeans with the sassy jewels all over them and that lacey black top that gives everyone a little peek of the girls. No; on second thought, the black top might be too much for an 'in' night. Tight T-shirt."

Rick gives her a little wink and the hand wave to signal her to get going. Jackie rolls her eyes and trudges upstairs.

Jackie wants to kill Rick and Tom. She loves them. They are fabulous cooks and the best friends and neighbors a girl could have. However, it is already 7:45 p.m., which means they are not eating until 9:00 p.m. at the earliest, and it's Friday. She hates having to be entertaining and engaging on Fridays. She is so much better on Saturdays. She is usually just so spent from her week that she much prefers a glass of a good red, a little Ben and Jerry's, and her couch. Ah, but that is also the control freak in her, always wanting things her way and to happen when she wants them to happen. It is just a trip downstairs; and if it is awful, she will just let out a few well-timed yawns, walk up one flight of stairs, and be home free.

Jackie unlocks her door, walks into her foyer, and smells the fresh, clean scent. *Thank goodness, I do not have to do any quick cleanups just in case the boys suddenly, and rather obviously, want to show their "friend" the view from my roof deck,* Jackie thinks to herself, feeling a bit of relief. She sometimes feels as though having a cleaning person twice a month is an extravagance. However, on days like today, she feels it is the best $150 she spends every month. To come home twice a month, on a Friday, to a clean house is heaven!

Now, typically, Jackie would spend some significant time on the primping—heck, she would probably even go out and make a new purchase, because, really, it is a first date; and even though she has been on, unfortunately, probably one thousand first dates, it is amazing that she never has an appropriate thing to wear for that particular first date. However, she has fifteen minutes, and she definitely wants time to get the story about this mystery man before he actually shows up. This is not the first time Tom and Rick have pulled a stunt like this; it is more like the tenth. And considering the history of their previous setups, Jackie is not getting her hopes up. You would think after four years of living next to each other—and, quite honestly, practically living with each other, the way they all spend time together—that these two would know her taste, but they do not. Jackie runs upstairs to her bedroom to change into Rick's suggested outfit. He is a gay man; she always takes his fashion advice. She throws on her bejeweled jeans, a black T-shirt, and some sassy black boots; it is winter, after all. She grabs her fleece jacket and runs up one more flight of stairs to smoke a quick cigarette before the real primping begins. Yes, she smokes. She knows she should not, and she is working on quitting; she's down to four a day during the week, but the number goes up a bit on weekends. She just has not yet been able to shake those four when she gets home from work.

She walks out onto her roof deck to the slight dusting of snow, stands out by the railing, and looks up and over to the Prudential Center, which is all lit up. She has an amazing view of Boston from her deck. It is her special spot. Not many can see her—well, that she knows of anyway—yet, she can look up at all of the buildings: the Prudential Center, the John Hancock, the series of brownstones behind her, and, on a clear day, she can catch a bit of downtown. It is her peace.

Well aware of her time constraints, Jackie does not go for her typical relaxed end-of-the-day cigarette. At this point, she is just going for the nicotine. She stomps it out in her ashtray, disguised as a flowerpot loaded with sand, and heads back inside. She runs into the bathroom and goes through the de-smoke routine: washes her face and hands, brushes her teeth, reapplies her makeup, hangs her head upside down and shakes out her long dark locks, flips, good, and off she goes. She pops into her kitchen as she is heading out her door and grabs the ever-traded-back-and-forth bottle of wine. Jackie can hear the music coming from Tom and Rick's apartment as she heads down the stairs; she doesn't even bother to knock. They know she is coming, and from the music they are playing, one of her favorite songs, they are not expecting her to knock.

"Hello," she yells as she walks down the hallway toward their rather fabulous open-concept kitchen, living room, and dining room. Their front layout is similar to hers. Hers is actually bigger, but in all honesty, these are two men who have fabulous taste and an incredible eye for decor. Their place rocks!

Tom pops out from the kitchen to greet Jackie at the end of the hall. He is wearing a bright red bib apron over his light pink button-down shirt and fabulous designer jeans. He is shaking his hips with a sinister smile as he sways to the music and extends his hand to her and starts to sing aloud to the song. Jackie puts the wine bottle down on the counter top and happily accepts his gesture to dance. Tom grabs her hand pulls her close to him, and off they go. Jackie will be the first to admit that the man can dance, and so can she. Rick is always commenting on how great Jackie and Tom look on the dance floor and admits that, at times, he is a bit jealous. Truly, Jackie is the one who is jealous. Tom is a smart, wonderful man who can dance, who can cook, who is stunning, and who is so in love with Rick. Tom stands about six foot one, slender yet strong build, dirty blond hair, amazing green eyes, and rather olive skin. Blonds are not even Jackie's type; but Tom—he is off the charts. Tom and Jackie are dancing up a storm on the living room rug, doing spins and twists and grooving away, so into their dancing that they would not even know it if ten people walked into the room.

Rick hears the laughing as he leads Greg down the hall to the living room. Greg arrived a bit early, and Rick has been showing him the rest of the condo. Even though Rick, Tom, and Greg have been friends for years, they always go out for dinner; this is actually the first time Greg has ever been to their home. Rick turns to Greg, motioning him to be quiet. Greg and Rick sneak down the rest of the hall and peak around the corner to the living room. Rick flashes Greg a huge grin as if he had just won the lottery. They watch and Tom and Jackie groove to the music, and Rick glances back occasionally to try and read Greg's response. He is pleased with the reaction he sees.

Greg is initially unsure of why Rick wants him to be quiet and feels a bit uneasy at first, spying on the woman with whom he is supposedly being set up. But as soon as Greg catches a glimpse of the living room dancing, he can't believe his eyes. This woman and Tom move with such grace and yet are having the time of their lives, so it seems. All Greg can really see was a pair of fabulous jeans on this woman with a rocking body, and the hair—long, dark, unbelievable hair. Occasionally when Tom spins her around, Greg gets a quick glimpse of her face, which is as pretty as the first time he saw her, months ago while she was having lunch with Tom. What truly strikes him is how much fun she seems to be having in a living room with her neighbor, whom she sees all of the time. Greg needs to focus. He is here for one purpose and one purpose only, and he does not need emotions to complicate his plans.

Rick takes one more glance up at Greg and is pleased with Greg's facial expression. Rick feels as though that is enough temptation for now, and he starts to clap and walk in the direction of Tom and Jackie.

"Bravo, Bravo." Rick says. "God, you two should really think about taking this show on the road."

Tom gives Jackie one last dip to end the show as she kicks one leg out for the sake of dramatics. She looks over toward Rick and, horrified, quickly pulls herself up as she notices a pair of black pants behind him.

"Jackie, I want you to meet our friend Greg." Rick motions toward Greg. "Greg, this is Jackie, the dancing therapist."

Greg walks over to Jackie and extends his hand. "You are quite the dancer," he says. "It's a pleasure to meet you."

Jackie shakes Greg's hand, feeling her face becoming totally flushed. "Thank you. Likewise—and for the record, my face is flushed from the dancing, not from the complete and utter embarrassment I feel right now." She shoots Tom and Rick the *you are both dead later* look.

Greg is almost speechless as he is now face to face with Jackie, who literally takes his breath away. "Embarrassment would be if I had been dancing; you two, unbelievable."

"Well, then," Rick interrupts the moment, giving Jackie an *I told you so* glance, "what can I get everyone to drink?"

Everyone follows Rick over to the island in the kitchen with a magnificent granite countertop, perfectly dressed with appetizers, glasses, and wine. Greg reaches over to the bottle of wine Jackie brought and notices the tic marks all over it. "What is this?"

"Ah," Tom says as he shoots Jackie a grin, "this is how we do it here. Rick, Jackie, and I decided that it is ridiculous to continue to bring wine over to each other's homes every time we get together. We get together a lot. So Jackie, being the creative creature she is, came up with this wonderful concept. We have one bottle of wine that we continually bring back and forth, but we never open it. Each time the wine is brought to your house, you get a tic mark. Jackie gets one and a half per time because, well, there is usually one of her and two of us. At the end of the year, whoever has the least amount of tic marks has to buy a great bottle for the three of us to share and a new tracking bottle for the next year."

"Really?" Greg responds. "That's a great idea. Who is winning?"

"They are," says Jackie. "What can I say? The boys are better cooks."

"Ah, yes, that is true. I mean, Jackie can cook, but we are better," Rick quips.

"Who is better?" Tom chimes in.

"Well, you are. But no one, and I mean no one, can top Jackie's desserts," Rick responds with yet another proud-of-himself glance toward Jackie.

Greg just smiles and looks over at Jackie. He holds the glance so long she is almost uncomfortable. However, she does not back down; she is always up for the challenge.

They all sit down to another fabulous meal that Tom has prepared; they laugh and drink wine, and it really is quite the perfect evening. Greg turns out to be an excellent conversationalist, which is not at all surprising as he is a vice-president of sales for a pharmaceutical company. He is also, from what Jackie can gather by how his clothes fit, in shape and has amazingly strong hands.

"Don't you, Jackie?" Rick's question pops her out of her moment in her head thinking about the handsome man sitting across from her.

"I'm sorry, Rick, what?" she replies.

"Girl, where were you? Don't you have the best view from your deck?"

"It is a nice view, I'll admit."

"Good; then let's go check it out."

Before Jackie can even respond, Rick gets everyone up, tops off the wine glasses on the way out, and upstairs they go. Jackie swears they love to do this to her. If they think she is even the slightest bit interested in someone, they conveniently come up with some excuse—usually the view from her deck—and manage to get everyone up to her place. Now, they never just disappear and leave her alone with the stranger whom she just met. They do, however, manage to get her on the deck alone with said stranger as they wait downstairs in her living room. They always seem to come up with some excuse as to why they can't go upstairs, and Jackie knows tonight's excuse will be that it is just too cold. And did she call it, or what? Rick and Tom plop down on her sofa and motion Jackie and Greg to go upstairs.

Greg and Jackie head up to the roof deck. The sky has now cleared, and the view is rather delightful.

"Wow, this is a good view," Greg says as he leans himself against the rail facing the Prudential Center.

Jackie stands next to Greg, just looking straight ahead at the night sky, "Thank you. Yes, unfortunately it is a bit chilly, or I would have everyone up here for a nightcap."

"Listen, Jackie," Greg says as he turns toward her, "I know this is an awkward but completely fun setup on Tom and Rick's part. I'll be honest, I never really like these fabricated situations. But I've had a great time tonight, and I would love to take you to dinner sometime."

"I'd love to," she replies.

"Great. Well, let's get you inside, it is cold. Beautiful, though."

"Yes, I am a lucky girl to have this view."

"I wasn't talking about the skyline."

Jackie looks back, and Greg is just smiling, motioning her inside the door. She smiles back, without a word, and heads inside.

Safely in the warmth of her apartment, they all sit in her living room on her swanky modern, yet comfortable, furniture that rests on old wide-pine floors. She has one exposed brick wall that, again, contrasts nicely with her modern furniture choices. The other walls are tastefully flanked with some thought-provoking black-and-white photographs. They finish their wine and all decide to part for the evening. Jackie walks the men to the door and gets her hugs and kisses from Tom and Rick. As the boys walk out ahead of Greg, Greg turns, gently grabs her hand, gives her a kiss on the cheek, and says, "See you soon." She shuts the door and heads over to clean up the glasses. *Interesting*, she thinks. *Greg is really sweet, smart, and handsome.* However, she doesn't have that kid-in-a-candy-store feeling she usually gets when she meets someone like him. There's something different about him; she just can't put her finger on it. Jackie does not waste much time thinking about it; she figures it was probably just the awkwardness of the blind setup.

LAUREN

"Honey, I'm home," Lauren calls out mockingly as she walks into the mudroom of her friends Olivia and Tommy's home.

"Hey there!" Olivia calls out from the kitchen. "Come on in."

Lauren peels off her layers of clothes and kicks off her hiking boots. She is dressed casually in jeans and a sweater, as it is December and freezing and she really did not feel the need to dress up for a Saturday evening preholiday dinner party with her lifelong friends who live in suburbia. She hates the fact that she had to leave the city on such a freezing-cold night, but without any alternative plans, she figured, why not make the trek from Boston down to Westwood?

Her friends are all married with children, living in the quintessential suburban towns surrounding Boston. Her friends all drive nice SUVs and have two to three children. They have moved on from play dates and Gymboree. They now have carpool obligations and weekend-long soccer tournaments to attend. Their kids have their own Facebook pages. The boys are getting taller and their voices deeper, and the girls are growing more beautiful and full of attitude. Lauren can't believe they all live such adult lives. These people, the ones she went to college with all those years ago. These people, whose main focus was hosting the best keg party and consuming the most upside-down kamikazes. These people are now responsible for raising kids. It is quite impressive to Lauren how they have all matured and become such productive members of society. It also makes her a bit sad. She always feels remorse that she is not raising her own children with her closest friends. If she ever has children, the others will be well into high school—and some in college. That is something that sits like a dull ache in her heart, but it is what it is; she is lucky to live close by and still be able to enjoy time with all of her friends and their families.

Lauren walks into the kitchen to see Olivia finishing up last-minute touches for the meal. Tommy, Rachel, and Eric are all sitting at the kitchen table, relaxed and sipping on cocktails. These are four of Lauren's favorite people. She has known them all for at least twenty years, and she always feels as at home and comfortable walking into either of their homes as she does her own. Lauren does not feel the need to entertain; she does not have to hide her emotions—well, for the most part. She doesn't have to keep the conversation flowing or constantly analyze what is going on in the room. She is not trying to impress anyone or sell herself and feels as though she can relatively be herself. She compliments Olivia on how wonderful it smells. Tommy gets up to give Lauren a kiss and get her something to drink. As Lauren heads over to kiss Eric and Rachel hello, she notices it is oddly quiet. "Wait!" Lauren stops and looks suspiciously around the kitchen. "How come I don't hear children?"

"Well, our kids are at Grandma's, and their kids are at their aunt's house," explains Rachel.

"Nice. But then, why am I here, instead of all of us having a night out in the city?"

"I'm with you on that, Lauren; I asked the same question." Tommy gives a look to Rachel.

"What?" exclaims Rachel. "Don't blame me; your wife is the one who wanted to cook."

"Ah," Lauren interrupts before the bickering starts so early in the evening, "this is great. I can't remember the last time I had a home-cooked meal."

"Have you even been eating? You look awfully skinny," Olivia snidely remarks.

"Yes, Mom, I've been eating; just stress."

"Work busy?" Tommy asks as he places a glass of wine in front of Lauren.

"Thank you. Yes, work is very busy—which hey, is a good thing. But I am exhausted, and I am really quite sick of dealing with the bridezillas."

"You know," Rachel quips, "not every bride is a 'zilla, and not every marriage is doomed for failure."

Lauren rolls her eyes. "When have I ever said every marriage is doomed for failure? Perhaps I am a bit jaded. I wonder why?" Lauren sarcastically puts her finger to her chin as if she is really trying to come up with some reasons. "Could it be that I have seen a few too many brides-to-be emasculate their future husbands in public, and a few grooms-to-be treat their future brides like complete idiots? Or maybe the twelve different times I have accidentally caught future brides and grooms making out with some other person at a bar?" Lauren pauses for the concurring head nods from her friends. "Seriously, though, who am I to judge? I am the queen serial dater."

"Yeah, speaking of which, no date tonight?" Olivia sarcastically asks while giving Lauren a perplexed look.

"No, not tonight. I had one last night, and I am having dinner with the finance dude tomorrow night."

"Gees, Lauren, how do you keep them straight?" asks Eric.

"Hey, a girl's gotta eat."

"I guess; to each her own," Eric smugly replies.

Eric can drive Lauren crazy. He has been with Rachel for over twenty years. He has never had to date as a true adult and has no idea what it is like to be dating at forty-two. Sometimes he makes the snidest remarks, and they are like a dagger in Lauren's heart. No one would like more to be in a healthy, normal relationship than Lauren; it just hasn't worked out that way. She hates having to go to bed by herself every night. She hates having to go on first date after first date, night after night. And to top it off, by day, she has to pretend how perfectly happy she is as she works with her brides- and grooms-to-be. She never imagined her life would look like this, and she hates it. She wants to rip his head off but instead does her usual humorous deflection. "Variety is the spice of life, my friend."

"Whatever happened to that Greg guy you were seeing? He seemed nice," Rachel says, trying to divert attention from her husband's comments.

Lauren shoots Olivia a here-we-go-again look. Lauren just wants to hang out, not be quizzed on her love life. "I don't know, actually. He got really busy with work, traveling a lot; and we stayed in touch and went out when he was in town, but he just kind of went away. I haven't heard from him since July."

"What do you mean, he just went away? You two were quite smitten for a bit; you went to the Bahamas in June. How can he just go away?" Rachel asks in a very judgmental tone.

"I have asked myself that same question more than you know, Rachel. Trust me."

Rachel is now getting a bit angry at the situation and the lack of answers. "Well, have you called him? Have you asked him? I don't understand."

"Rachel, you have been married for almost twenty years. I do not expect you to understand what it is like to date at forty-two. May we please just talk about something else?" Lauren asks wearily.

Lauren takes a swig of her wine. She can't blame Rachel for her confusion. She herself was just as confused by Greg's sudden disappearance. She does not want to have to admit just how many phone calls, text messages, and e-mails went unanswered. She does not want to admit just how crazy it made her feel and how those last few e-mails she sent were actually crazy rants. What can she do? She has learned…well, no, actually, she has not learned. She's trying to learn and accept that as you get older, in the dating world, things make less and less sense. She tries constantly and consciously to let things go and learn from her behavior and from others. There is, however, something left over from her relationship with Greg that haunts her, something far beyond her crazy e-mails. She does not even know how to talk about it with anyone. In her gut, she feels she may have done something terribly wrong.

EVA

"Boy, it is a cooold morning."

Eva's lost in her thoughts, staring blankly straight ahead as she waits in the taxi line at Logan Airport, when suddenly her red-eye-induced trance is interrupted.

"Sure is a cold morning."

Eva looks up at the man standing in front of her. He is tall and rather attractive, with a slight southern drawl.

"It is," Eva replies to the gentleman, "Welcome to Boston."

"Are you here on business too?" he asks.

"No, I actually live here, just returning from a business trip."

"Well, I hear this is a great city; but me being from the South, I do not like my welcome so far."

"How long are you here for?"

"All week—I leave next Saturday. I need to be in my own home for the holidays."

"Well, I wish I could tell you it will warm up, but it probably won't. Just bundle up and enjoy Boston from inside high places."

The gentleman laughs. "I am Stephen, by the way," he says as he extends his bare hand.

Eva reaches out to shake his hand, "Eva. Nice to meet you. And might I suggest you get yourself some gloves."

The cab pulls up, and Stephen is about to head to it, but he turns to Eva first and says, "I may be out of line, but I am in town all week. I would love it if you could join me for dinner, perhaps show me the fun stuff in Boston."

Of course you would, Eva thinks to herself. "I really don't know my schedule."

"Well," the man says as he reaches into his overcoat pocket and hands his business card to Eva, "here is my number, just in case you find yourself with a free night. I'm a Southern gentleman—just dinner, no expectations."

Eva smiles and accepts the card, thinking, *Of course there aren't any expectations*. She wants to do a complete eye roll but instead thanks him and says she will call if she is free. She throws her luggage into the open trunk of the next cab and jumps into the cab, desperate to get out of the bitterly cold, dry air. "Two-fifty Beacon Street, please."

Eva gazes out the window on the drive home. Even though it is blustery outside, the sun is shining brightly. She is debating whether to try and get a few hours of sleep or just push through to Sunday and crash by 8:00 p.m. The red-eye always seems like a good idea at the time, but it never really is. The cab pulls up to her building, and the driver pops out and grabs here suitcase. Eva tips him well and then heads inside.

"Welcome home, Miss Eva."

"Hi, Tommy. Thank you."

"Did you have a nice trip?" he asks.

"I did. Tommy, thank you. Did I miss anything exciting?"

"No, no; just a lot of cold weather and some snow, as you can see."

Eva heads through her building lobby and on to the elevator, where she pushes the penthouse button with a smile on her face. She loves her doorman, Tommy; he is one of the nicest people and probably the one person she sees most often in her life. She walks into her stunning three-bedroom penthouse apartment. Her large windows give her a fabulous view of the Charles River. Her place is perfect and modern—and now very clean as the housekeepers came while she was away. She rolls her suitcase into her bedroom and flops onto her king-size bed. *I missed you, bed,* she thinks to herself. It would be nice to just crawl in, but instead Eva decides to leave her suitcase packed for now. She throws on her running clothes and heads out for an easy ten-mile run through the city.

Running is Eva's sanity. She reserves her long runs for when she is actually home, but she still manages, even with her crazy travel schedule, to run four to five miles, five days a week. The air is cold as it hits her lungs, but running in the winter feels so good to Eva. And it is much easier to get used to the cold air on the lungs than the heavy, humid air that comes with the Boston summers. Eva gets into a zone while running and just lets her mind run freely. Sometimes she thinks about possible solutions to work issues; sometimes she thinks about retiring and where she would like to go. Sometimes she just thinks about her life; those are the usually the thoughts that make her runs long and hard.

Eva knows most people think she is cold, but she is not; she has just had so tragedies in her life, and things so often go awry. She finds most relationships quite trivial. She decided years ago to focus on her career, as it is something she can, for the most part, control and set herself up for a great life later. She has done all of that. She owns a multimillion-dollar condo outright; she has five million in the bank and another two million in retirement. Yet, she still can't quite give up her job. She complains about it—about the isolation, the hours in airports, and countless nights in hotel rooms. But it has become her purpose, the one consistency in her life. What would she do if she quit? What would she do if she woke up on a Monday morning and was actually home, without any travel on the horizon?

I guess I am about to find out, Eva thinks to herself, *no thanks to my therapist or me.* Eva has been seeing a therapist for six months now, on and off. Her therapist asked her to join a group for six weeks as she feels Eva is stuck, and group work may be beneficial for her. So Eva has agreed to arrange her schedule so she is home for six long weeks. Eva is a vice-president of strategic development, so it was not an easy task to accomplish. It just so happened that her CEO asked her to oversee a project in Boston for the next two months. The job will be consuming most of her time, so she does not have a single trip planned for two months. *Funny how things work out.* Eva smiles. But she is also panicked. Panicked about the group, panicked about staying in one place. She knows she wants out of her job and career, but then what? All of this torments Eva, but what torments her the most is getting through the next two weeks. It is the week before Christmas; she is wrapping up her last project for the year and will not begin her next one until after the New Year. She is home for two weeks without any focus.

After finishing her run, Eva turns on the coffee maker and jumps into the shower. She loves the postrun high and can't wait to sit down with a warm cup of coffee. She pours herself a cup and opens her refrigerator. *Shit, nothing. Shit, no creamer, no food, nothing.*

SHELLY

Shelly walks into her favorite local pub at five thirty on Tuesday night just days before Christmas. She brushes off the snow as she pulls off her hat and gloves. She glances around at the half-full bar and gives a wave and a smile to the bartender. This is her local pub; most days she knows most of the people in the pub, but not today, not just a few days before Christmas. Her local pub has become a maze of unknown Newbury street shoppers who have filtered down Mass Avenue to Beacon Street. She stares blankly at the unknown masses.

"Shelly!" Shelly hears her name being called and looks over to the center of the room. Sitting at a round high-top are three of her friends, Megan, Kevin, and Tim, all of whom live in or near her building. These are friends she has made over the last few years while living in her neighborhood. They are all young—four to six years younger than she—single, and professional. Shelly quickly learned that even though she is thirty-eight, she, too, is a single professional and needs to have similar friends for nights such as this, where you just want to go out and grab a drink or a quick bite, but yet, not alone.

Shelly starts to strip her coat off as she heads over to join her friends. She gives out kisses on the cheek to each of her friends before she grabs a seat. Just as she sits, the bartender comes over with a glass of pinot noir and sets it down in front of her.

"Lindsey, you are the best; thank you."

"It is what we do, Shelly, for those we know and love," Lindsey replies she blows Shelly an air kiss and heads back to tend to her bar.

Shelly raises her glass, and her friends follow suit. "A toast, on the night before, the night before, the two nights before Christmas; may we enjoy our chill time now and rely on it later to survive the craziness of this season."

EVA

It is Christmas Eve, and Eva is finishing up her work for the year. Her cell phone rings, and she sees it is her CEO. "Hi, John. Merry Christmas."

"Eva, how is my favorite person on the planet?"

Eva laughs. "I am well; just closing out the final details for the year."

"Do you know how much money you made us this year, Eva? You made us lots and lots of money, Eva!"

"I have a good idea, John."

"Well, Eva, again, you set a new standard, and I don't think you will be unhappy with the four-million-dollar bonus the partners just approved."

Eva was shocked; she was used to getting one or two million dollars; even though she knows how well she did, four million dollars is unprecedented.

"Eva…" John says over the phone, making sure she is still there.

"John. Wow, I am shocked; that is amazing. Thank you."

"No need to thank me, Eva; we love you, and you are one of the most dedicated, income-producing employees this company has ever had. I'm serious, Eva; you are one of the smartest, most creative individuals I have ever met. I just really, really appreciate everything you do. You need to know that."

"Well, John, that bonus certainly says so," says Eva. "And hey, I appreciate working for someone like you. There are very few ethical CEOs left in this business, and I am glad I work for one of them."

"So are you heading to New Hampshire to be with your family?" John deflects, as he has never been good at accepting compliments.

Eva pauses for a second. "Ah, yes, leaving tonight. I plan on being there for a few days—but not to worry, I will close out all of the Brioche Technology numbers for the year, and I will be back by the New Year and ready to take on our next challenge."

"That's my girl! Oh, and Eva, don't worry too much about the final numbers. We will probably need you to continue with Brioche Technologies for another month or so. At least until we get the approval. All my best to your family, Eva; I wish I could call them myself and thank them for raising such a fantastic woman. I hope they are as proud of you as I am."

"Thank you, John. They are. And my love to Bunny and the kids, and enjoy the tropical weather!"

"Oh I will, Eva. Merry Christmas."

"Merry Christmas, John, and thank you."

Eva hangs up the phone, sits back, and takes a deep breath. Her emotions are torn; she questions whether she should cry tears of joy or complete sadness. She made $5,000,000. She is all too well aware that what she made in one year is five times what the average American dreams of making in a lifetime. Eva gets up and walks out onto her large balcony overlooking the Charles River. The weather has warmed up to forty-five degrees. It is 4:00 p.m., and the sun is going down. She watches the brave crewmembers rowing along the Charles. She breathes in the mild air.

This is the neighborhood she coveted as an adolescent. She remembers taking the number eight bus to Kenmore and walking around the beautiful Back Bay streets and thinking, *Someday*. And now, she is here: all set, no mortgage, no financial worries, living in luxury in the most beautiful part of her city. Yet, she is as lonely as she was as a teenager, on those days when she would come into town and worship the neighborhood where she now resides. As a teenager she often thought that if she could only get here, things would be different. Things are different. They are much different; yet, still, she is just as lonely.

Eva will not be heading to New Hampshire tonight to see her made-up family. She will be staying in by herself. Tomorrow she will head down to a homeless shelter for women and children and serve meals and bring presents for the kids. Eva continues to stare at the Charles, feeling a bit guilty for lying to John about her *family* in New Hampshire. She closes her eyes and pushes back the terrifying thoughts that begin to seep into her mind. She walks back into her house, puts on her running clothes, and off she goes, without a tear shed.

Just days before Christmas, Eva bought herself a case of very expensive wine. She laughs as she looks at her wine rack and realizes she has ten bottles left. *Ten days home by myself, ten bottles of a good red, perfect.* Eva opens a bottle, pours a glass, raises her glass, and says, "Here is to still having plenty of wine to get through these torturous nights." After her run, she showers, applies makeup, and puts on her jeans and a great top. Eva celebrates yet another night by herself, Christmas Eve. She heads out to her balcony to smoke a cigarette. She laughs to herself as she lights up her cigarette. People have always acted so shocked when they find out she smokes, as she is such an avid runner. She inhales and slowly lets out the smoke and, with it, the stress of her day, her year, and her life. *A runner who smokes is not even close to representing the enigma I truly am.*

LAUREN

"Who the hell gets married on Christmas Eve? I mean really, talk about not having any consideration for others," Lauren's assistant exclaims as she meticulously adjusts the table centerpieces the florist just delivered.

"Maria, it will be fine," Lauren calmly replies, although she is in complete agreement. "Look, I just need your help until five in the afternoon, when the bride starts marching down the aisle. As soon as she does, you are free to go, my friend."

Maria continues to run from table to table, making adjustments and continuing to rant about the Christmas Eve wedding. "I know it will be fine, and I will stay as long as you want. But Lauren, it's not fair to you, either; now you can't go home until tomorrow, and I hate that you are going to be going home late, by yourself, on Christmas Eve."

"Maria, I am a grown woman. I will be fine, and tomorrow I will be with my family. Besides, if it were not for this wedding, I would not be able to give you this." Lauren hands Maria a card. "Merry Christmas Maria, I really could not do any of this without you."

Maria stops and opens the card that reads, "Merry Christmas, Maria. I hope you and Matt have a fabulous four days. I wish I could give you more because you are worth a million. Thank you for everything you do. Love, Lauren." Maria gasps when she sees a bonus check for $10,000. Her mouth drops open, and her eyes begin to fill with tears. She runs over and gives Lauren the biggest hug.

"Oh, my God, Lauren, thank you, thank you, thank you! This is unbelievable!"

"You're welcome!" Lauren says as she returns Maria's hug.

Both women are smiling brightly, Maria because she has never received a check that big and Lauren for feeling as though she made Maria's day. They separate, and Lauren states, "All right, now let's stop thinking of this wedding as a pain in the ass and more of a ten-thousand-dollar bonus and get this show on the road."

Maria, who cannot stop smiling, goes right back to work with a spring in her step. The wedding goes off without any major trauma, and all seem happy and healthy. At about ten o'clock that night, most guests have slowly made their exit, and all who remain are the drunk and disorderly. At this point Lauren knows she can safely part, for the rest is in the hands of the hotel staff—and good luck to them.

Lauren bundles up. It was a warm December day; however, the sun set over five hours ago, and now the chill is significant, and the snow has started to come down. She exits the hotel lobby and heads down Newbury Street to Dartmouth. Lauren lives on a quiet Back Bay street in a great neighborhood; however, her street is dimly lit, and at this hour, with the city being so quiet, she thinks best to walk home on the major streets. She walks down Dartmouth and takes a left onto Commonwealth Avenue, stopping for a minute to take in the beauty of the "Comm Ave Mall" (as the locals call it), with all the trees lit up in white lights. The Comm Ave Mall runs down the middle of Commonwealth Avenue. It is a long, paved walking path that starts at Arlington Street and continues down through Kenmore Square. The walking path is lined on either side with grass, trees, and park benches. The Comm Ave Mall is broken up in sections by every cross street. And as one begins the journey down the Mall, one finds many historic statues and tributes. Lauren thinks to herself that for a small "big" city, they really make it look pretty.

Lauren continues down Commonwealth Avenue and then takes a right down Fairfield; then she takes a left onto Marlborough Street, and within three steps, she is at her front door. Marlborough Street is lined by the typical Boston brownstones and runs parallel to and between Beacon Street and Commonwealth Avenue; however, Marlborough is a narrower, one-way street, so there is less traffic. She unlocks the main door and hikes up three flights of stairs to her apartment, one floor shy of the "penthouse" level. She unlocks her door, flips on the light, and throws her keys on her multifunctioning kitchen cart. Sometimes it is used as a cooking space, but most of the time, it is used to collect her keys, mail, and anything else she has in her hands when she walks in the door.

Lauren's apartment is not modern by any means. However, it is a good-sized two-bedroom with lots of character and a small deck off her living room. She absolutely loves her apartment—and the rent even more. She would love to own a place of her own someday; however, the prices of apartments are so high in Boston that it is just not in the cards at this time. She is patient and knows her business and reputation are growing every year. Someday she will have the money to own her own little piece of the Back Bay; *until then*, she thinks, *this doesn't suck*. Lauren pours a glass of wine from the open bottle that has been sitting on her counter for days, flips on the news, and tries to unwind from the busy week. Lauren is so exhausted she does not even care that it is Christmas Eve.

JACKIE

Jackie closes her office door as her last patient for the day exits. It is 1:00 p.m. on Christmas Eve, and it took everything she had to stay focused during her last session. Ironically, Jackie, who during this time of year does a great deal of education on stress reduction for her clients, is ready to jump out of her skin. She has not started her shopping, she has to purchase some sort of food product to bring to her parents' house in the morning, and she has date number three with Greg tonight. She sits at her desk and leans back in her leather chair and wishes she actually did have that magic wand her patients often expect her to have. She would love to wave it ceremoniously through the air, have all of her shopping done, food ready to go, and be wearing the perfect third date outfit. She looks out her office window to the brownstones across the street. She smiles as she thinks about seeing Greg tonight. She had such a great time with him on their first and second dates. She realizes she is beginning to actually like him, and time flies by when they are together. She wonders if tonight he will actually kiss her. *God, I hope so,* she thinks to herself. Jackie realizes she could sit in her chair for hours daydreaming; however, as she does not have a magic wand and only a mere five hours to get everything done before she is to meet Greg, she had best get a move on.

By 5:00 p.m. Jackie has miraculously managed to get all of her shopping done and presents wrapped…well, placed in bags with tags, anyway. She is showered and dressed, and with an hour to spare. She stands in her kitchen looking at her living room, which suddenly appears very festive due to all of the holiday gift bags lined up along one wall. Jackie is not much of a holiday decorator. She does not have a tree, but she does manage to buy a few poinsettias and throw some pretty blue-and-white bulbs in glass vases so that she does not appear to be a complete Grinch. She does; however, have a stuffed Grinch in a Santa outfit, which she proudly displays, as it is her favorite decoration of all time. She takes in the peace and considers pouring a glass of red, bundling up, and sitting on her deck for a smoke, when a knock and a "Hello, love" interrupt her trance.

"Hi, Rick. Merry Christmas, love."

Rick comes bouncing in, very pleased to see Jackie is home. "Oh, thank God, Jackie. I need a quick pep talk before I head off to Tom's parents' house."

"You mean you would like a glass of wine and a cigarette."

Rick purses his lips and pretends as if he is holding back the tears, "Jackie, I just love that you understand me." He gives Jackie a quick kiss on the cheek and reaches over her to grab two wine glasses; he places them on the counter and looks at Jackie. "Start pouring, girl."

Rick is not a daily smoker; he is the occasional smoker. He occasionally smokes when he drinks and occasionally smokes when he is nervous or stressed out. He is the guy all smokers wishes they could be and secretly hate. Jackie pours some wine in each glass; they throw on coats and head upstairs to the smokers' lounge. Jackie does have two Adirondack chairs that she keeps cleared of snow for those winter nights that are warm enough to sit and smoke. And although it is supposed to get quite cold later in the evening, the day is sunny and mild, and the temperature is a balmy forty-five degrees. Jackie places her sand-filled flowerpot ashtray between the two chairs, and she and Rick sit down and simultaneously let out a big sigh of relief.

"So, Rick, why do you always get so tense before you go to Tom's parents' house? They love you."

"I don't know, Jackie, I just do; no real reason. Don't get me wrong, I adore his family; they are just so formal and just different from mine. It's really not a big deal; I mean, tomorrow morning Tom has to suffer through my crazy-ass family. It's just nice to have a bit of chill time before we head over."

"I know the holidays make everyone crazy, or sad, or depressed, or something other than normal. I don't even know why we put ourselves through it year after year."

"Amen to that." Rick leans his glass into Jackie's. "Speaking of which, we have our annual reservation tomorrow night, Mistral, at seven o'clock."

"Yay!" Jackie stomps her feet. "I can't wait!"

Every year Jackie, Rick, and Tom celebrate Christmas night together at a restaurant. They do not exchange gifts; they just enjoy a fantastic meal together that no one has to cook, and they all have a chance to exhale without having to put on any airs."

"Oh!" Rick exclaims. "Wait, do I need to change the reservation from three to four?"

"No! I am going out with Greg tonight. And thank you. You boys did a very good job this time."

"We try. So is this date three?"

"It is. I'm excited, Rick; he seems like a really great guy. How did this all happen, by the way?"

"What do you mean?"

"I mean, what made you two think of setting us up? It sounds like you have all known each other for a while, and I have never heard you or Tom mention him."

"Really? We've never mentioned him. Gosh, it seems like we have been meaning to set you two up for a while. How did that all come about? Wait, I know this; let me think for a second." Rick places one hand to his forehead as if doing so will magically bring the answer to the front of his mind.

"It is not a big deal, Rick; I was just curious."

"No, Jackie, there is a story to this, and it is a good one. I just don't want to mess it up. I remember timing being an issue. What was it? Oh, I know—he knew you."

"Knew me? What?" Jackie was totally taken back by that statement. She had never seen Greg until she met him at Rick and Tom's apartment.

"No, not knew you; he saw you," explains Rick. "Yes, that's it. He saw you once having lunch or something with Tom."

"He did?"

"Yeah, I think he saw you leaving or something. It was a long time ago, Jackie. But the point is…oh, um, maybe I shouldn't say."

"Shouldn't say what?"

"Jackie, I am going to ruin it."

"Ruin what?" she asks. "Right now you are just freaking me out."

"Exactly, I am ruining it."

"Keep talking, Rick."

"Ugh, Tom is going to kill me. OK, Greg saw you having lunch or something with Tom, and you had left, and then Greg went to speak with Tom, and he asked Tom about you. So he thought you were cute. It was months ago, like last spring or summer. Anyway, he was just getting out of a relationship and traveling a lot. He always seemed to be in Chicago or California. Tom and I made the executive decision to give it some time before we introduced the two of you because we thought you two made a good pair. There, I said it, we controlled the situation. I am sorry, Jackie."

Jackie grins. "No need to apologize, Rick; that is sweet. And, I must say, probably smart of you two to give him some time to exit a relationship properly. Thank you. And you are right, he does spend a lot of time in Chicago and California, but that just lets me focus on my work during the week."

Rick just smiles, half because he is proud of himself and half because he is so happy to see that smile on Jackie's face. Jackie and Rick sit, chat, and smoke for another ten minutes, and then both suddenly realize their excess time has quickly drained and now they both have to rush off, Rick to Tom's parents' house and Jackie to her date.

Jackie takes a quick glance at the clock as she races out the door. She realizes she has fifteen minutes to make it to the restaurant and decides walking is faster than trying to get a cab. She starts briskly walking down Dartmouth Street to Commonwealth Avenue. Greg has picked a quiet, casual Tapas restaurant that not many people know about. It is off the beaten path, so it tends to be less crowded than those on Newbury or Boylston streets. Jackie is so happy with this choice. She did not want to be around all of the hustle and bustle; she just wanted a quiet corner table to herself. Well, she just wanted Greg to herself.

On her walk she ponders the idea of confronting Greg about seeing her prior to them actually meeting. She decides against it. Why would she embarrass Greg like that, or even worse, jeopardize a relationship between Greg, Rick, and Tom? Details can just be too complicating; there is no need to bring something so innocent out into the open. She should just accept the compliment and let things unfold. It is kind of romantic, when Jackie thinks about it. Greg was interested enough to ask a friend and patient enough to wait to be set up with her.

Jackie walks down the steps and enters the restaurant; she takes a quick glance at the people seated to her left, nods to the hostess, and then heads toward the bar. She quickly sees Greg as he stands up from a side bar table he had nabbed. Greg reaches out to Jackie as she starts to apologize for being a bit late; he kisses her softly on the lips and then wraps his arms around her and whispers, "Merry Christmas." Jackie could stand there all night in his embrace. He just calmed her down in two seconds flat; no one has ever been able to calm her down like that. They spent the next four hours chatting and laughing, drinking Sangria, and ordering small plate after small plate. Greg holds her hand, rubs her leg, and is constantly doing small things that let her know he is completely focused on her. By ten o'clock they decide to call it a night as they both have to be up early to travel to visit their families. Greg insists on walking Jackie home as the city had become quite sparse on this Christmas Eve.

As they near Jackie's street corner, Greg stops and grabs her around the waist. "Jackie," he says, half laughing, "as corny as this sounds, this has been the best Christmas Eve ever."

Jackie throws her head back, laughing. "Greg, that is a totally corny line, but I agree. And we are both cheese balls."

Greg lets out a laugh, lets go of her, grabs her hand, and keeps walking. It is romantic; the city is lit up beautifully, and the snow is falling. When they reach Jackie's brownstone, Greg stops again, grabs her waist, and pulls her against him. He puts one hand on her face and gently strokes her cheek with his thumb. Without losing eye contact, Greg leans down and softly kisses Jackie on the lips. Greg pulls his lips off Jackie's for a second, but his face is still touching hers; she feels his breath, his thumb still stroking her cheek. His lips touch hers again, softly, then a bit more passionately; he opens his mouth as his tongue gently searches for hers, yet his arm around her waist gets tighter, pulls her closer, and she can feel his hand move from her cheek to the back of her head, pulling her in closer to his face. They continue this dance of gentle lips and tongues, yet the strong arms and grips represent the fiery passion that has been ignited. They both pull away simultaneously to catch their breath. Greg pulls Jackie against him again, and she rests her head on his chest. "Holy shit," she says, breathless.

Greg kisses her forehead and smiles in such a way that she can feel his smile. He wraps his arms around her more tightly.

"I wish I didn't have to go," Greg whispers, "but if I kiss you again, I will never leave."

Jackie lets out a pouting moan. She pulls her head off his chest, reaches her hands up, and cradles his face. "I know," she states. She kisses him, and still holding his face, she smiles and says, "Merry Christmas."

Greg kisses her again. "That it is, Jackie. Now, get inside; you know I'm not going to leave until your door is locked behind you. I'll call you in the morning."

Greg does just as he says; he waits until Jackie is safely behind her building doors before he turns to leave. He heads back toward Dartmouth Street for the better likelihood of catching a cab. Greg is still feeling the energy of their kiss running through his body. He is surprised by how much he likes Jackie. He is less surprised by how much he wants to sleep with Jackie. Greg tries to calm himself down. He knows he can't just sleep with Jackie like he has every other woman in his life. She is not just some woman. He knows there is a lot at stake. This situation is different. Jackie is different. He needs to play this differently.

SHELLY

Shelly decides it is Christmas Eve and she is going to treat herself to a holiday cocktail. She turns left as she walks out of her building on Beacon Street. She trudges up to Mass Ave and takes a right. She passes by a relatively dead bar on Mass Ave, heads up to Newbury Street, and takes a left. A few quick steps and Shelly finds herself peeling off her scarf and hat as she is greeted with a warm smile from the stunningly gorgeous young hostess at Sonsie.

Shelly takes a quick glance at the front tables and makes her way to the back. She finds one open stool at the bar. Shelly is amazed at how busy the bar is for Christmas Eve. She is greeted by yet another stunningly gorgeous young woman. Shelly decides to nickname her "Stunning."

"Hi, Merry Christmas. What can I get for you tonight?" asks the young woman.

At least Stunning is sweet, Shelly thinks to herself. "Well," she responds rather flirtatiously, "what do you recommend for a good, *strong* holiday treat?"

"I have just the drink," Stunning replies, equally flirtatious and respecting the single-girl code, "and if you don't like it, everything is on me!"

"Well, OK, I will try it," Shelly responds, all smiles. Then she thinks to herself, *Why can't men be this easy?*

Stunning returns with a martini glass, empty except for cranberries at the bottom and a green leaf that Shelly assumes is mint, and a small shaker. She pours a light pink drink into the martini glass and then tops it off with some champagne. Stunning watches intently as Shelly takes her first sip. Shelly's eyes widen. "Oh my, that is heaven and Christmas all in one! That is fabulous! By the end of the night, you will have to give me the recipe."

Stunning flashes Shelly a huge grin. "Yay, I am glad you like it. It is my own little concoction, and I will gladly share!"

Stunning runs off to tend to others at the bar, and Shelly happily takes another sip. She leans back in her bar stool to peek through the crowd to the wall of windows, and she sees what makes her breathe a sigh of relief: snowflakes beginning to fall. Shelly could not be happier. The big news in Boston has been an enormous Christmas storm beginning tonight and continuing on throughout Christmas Day. Shelly is grateful. She has the perfect excuse not to drive to Maine for the holiday. Her parents are relieved that their only daughter will not be driving in the snow but very concerned about her spending the day alone. Shelly had told them that she would be spending it with friends whose flights were canceled and making a great day of an otherwise very disappointing situation. She lied. She had to. She did not want her parents to worry about her or feel badly that she would actually be spending Christmas alone. She could be with friends; there were plenty of invitations, but she truly is not feeling the holiday spirit this year. She just wants to be alone and have it all just quietly pass by.

As Shelly comes to, realizing she has been staring out the window for a bit, her eyes scan the bar, and she notices an older man at the far corner of the bar staring at her. When he catches her eye, he smiles and raises his glass to her. She does not acknowledge him and quickly looks down and turns her head the opposite direction. She takes a sip of her drink. She is not sure why, but her eyes are drawn back over to the far corner of the bar. The older man is gone. A chill goes down her spine, one that actually makes her physically quiver.

EVA, CHRISTMAS DAY

Eva pours herself a cup of tea after returning to her apartment from the homeless shelter. She feels good after spending the morning assisting those who need it. She loved watching the children's eyes get wide with excitement opening up their presents. That is what makes her day. She does not care that she is spending Christmas alone. She always spends Christmas alone. She will continue to spend every Christmas alone if it means seeing those bright, wonderful, excited eyes. Seeing the children, who have had so much pain and suffering in their lives, light up as bright as the Christmas trees decorating the shelter makes Eva's day. Eva does her part for the shelter throughout the year. She shops for them when she can. She donates over $100,000 annually, and she always comes through for any special projects or issues that come up along the way. She gets letters, thank-you notes, and constant gratitude from the staff and the board. But, nothing, nothing is a bigger thank you to Eva than seeing a child's smile or the light in their eyes where there was none before. Eva sits on her couch, sips her tea, and lets herself take in the happiness of the day for a few more minutes.

Before long Eva is back to her usual self. It is 2:00 p.m. on Christmas Day, but there is work to be done. If she wants to keep giving to this shelter, she needs to keep producing. Eva saunters into her office and logs onto her computer. This is a perfect afternoon to get caught up on the numbers for Brioche Technologies. Even though there is still time before the year closes, Eva likes to get ahead of her projections, so she will not have any surprises.

By 7:00 p.m. Eva is still hard at work and now frantic. She has to be missing something. Nothing is right. The numbers are not making sense. "Shit," Eva says aloud as she pushes back from her desk. "Shit!" Eva reaches for the flip phone sitting on her desk and presses the number one.

A voice on the other picks up and says, "Merry, Merry Christmas, beautiful!"

"Hey, you, Merry Christmas." Eva is having a hard time masking her anxiety.

"Uh, oh, that is not the voice I want to hear. What is going on?"

"Can you come over? I think I found a problem, a huge problem."

"I will be there in thirty minutes."

SHELLY

"Last night I had a very bizarre dream. I was on the phone with my mother, who told me that my relatives in northern Maine saw a very large crocodile crossing their yard. Next thing I know, I was leaving some sort of gathering. I was in a familiar place, but I could not figure out where exactly I was. I got into a car that was already turned on, but the trick was, I could not turn the car off or really drive it; yet I was in the driver's seat and the car was set to only go so far. I knew this and got into the car anyway. The car drove me to a very secluded spot, again one that I was familiar with. I realized I was in my hometown in northern Maine. It was a very dark night, and I was alone. I started to panic, almost as if someone or something was chasing me, although, I was not certain who or what. I decided I had to run to the end of the very isolated road to the main road and try and catch a cab. (By the way, they do not have cabs in my hometown.) I was running as fast as I could and could feel the panic and fear rising in me as I started to come down a hill almost to the main road. All of a sudden, I stopped. I saw in front of me a crocodile crossing the road. This was not just any crocodile; this was a dream-sized, super huge, science fiction–style crocodile. Really, like the size of an eighteen-wheeler. I stopped dead in my tracks, knowing I had to back away before it saw me. I started to turn and run back up the hill in the direction of my house. I was completely panicked. I looked over my shoulder only to see the midsection of the crocodile starting to arch up as if it noticed me, and it was starting to turn toward my direction. I could not see its head; I could not see the end of its tail, just its massive midsection arching up to change direction. At that moment I was in a complete state of fear. I started to try to use my cell phone to call for help, but could not think of a number to dial. I suddenly realized, as the crocodile started to get closer to completing its turn toward me, that I was less than one-tenth of a mile from two of my relatives' homes and about a half a mile from the home I grew up in. For one second the panic left my body, and I thought to myself, *Why didn't you go to any of those places initially?* I looked back, and the crocodile had arched its back even more. It was almost as if its midsection was growing larger as it arched. The pure panic came rushing back into my body. And then I woke up. I awoke, sitting up in my bed, out of breath, my tank top completely soaked in sweat, and I was dazed and confused. I fell back on my pillow, catching my breath thinking to myself, *Please don't tell me I'm premenopausal; that would suck!"*

Chelsea was laughing hysterically on the other end of the phone. "Girl, that is a crazy dream. You're just stressed, and you're not premenopausal. You're thirty-eight for goodness' sake."

"Look, I'm just saying. That was my dream, and it was so real. It totally freaked me out. My therapist is going to love this one."

"How is your therapy going, and what the hell are you so stressed out about?"

"I don't know, Chelsea. I think I'm just in a rut with my job, and there are so many other things I would rather be doing, but none that I am certain would bring in the paycheck that I would need."

"Well, you must have some good coin saved. I mean, you make a good salary, you've been with them for ten years…just take the leap. Or, make a plan and save to take the leap if that is what you really want to do."

"Yeah, now you sound like my therapist. I don't know, I ebb and flow, as does everyone, else right?"

"True," says Chelsea. "I have those days as well—although usually about my marriage. Do I want to stay or go, stay or go?"

"Chelsea, come on, you love Eli."

"I do. But there are days, Shelly, as we both always say, when the grass is greener. Speaking of which, how are things going with Bill?"

"Bill? Well, you know, he ended it before Christmas."

"What? Why didn't you call me? I am sorry, girl; what a jerk!"

"It's fine. I was not that into him anyway, and we were what, dating a whole six weeks? On the bright side, he saved me the torture of buying a gift!"

"You sure? I know this time of year is hard. Especially up in Boston! And I am your best girl; don't lie to me, Shelly."

"Really, Chelsea, I am absolutely fine! Trust me, whom do I always call when I am heartbroken and about to eat my way through a tub of ice cream? Listen, I have to run. I'm starting group therapy in an hour, and I haven't done my prep work for it."

"Shocking—you, waiting until the last minute. Wait, what? Group therapy?"

"Yes, my therapist thinks a group would help me push through some areas she feels I am stuck in. Whatever; I'll give it a try."

"Well, let me know how that goes. Good luck; call me tomorrow."

"Will do."

Shelly hangs up the phone and heads over to her red high-back leather chair. She picks up her pen and notebook from the ottoman in front of her. She stares at the page that is blank except for, "If I had six months to live, what would I do? If I have lived my six months, what would I regret?" Shelly lets out a huge sigh. She has been trying to write this all weekend and cannot get beyond the title. She is now down to the wire and has one hour before she has to leave to go to her first group-therapy session. She gets up and paces around her small, quaint living room. Shelly is beating herself up verbally because, yet again, she has waited until the last minute—the story of her life. Yet, typically, she works so well under pressure; that is when she functions best. It's when she gets stuff done. But she is so stuck with this project that she can't understand it. Shelly knows exactly what the large crocodile represents in her life; she knows what is stressing her out every day. She just can't bring herself to face it.

Finally, Shelly sits back down and thinks to herself, *Screw it, just put anything down.* And that is what she does. Thirty minutes later, Shelly is relatively pleased with her 20 percent real, 80 percent bullshit response. She shoves her notebook in her Coach briefcase, tucks her jeans into her Ugg boots, and throws on her camel-colored designer coat. She reaches up into her closet; pulls down her basket full of winter gear; digs through to find matching white cashmere hat, gloves, and scarf; and off she goes.

SESSION 1

It is 5:30 p.m., and Jackie checks her voice mails. She is surprised but greatly relieved to not have any cancellations from her group members. Tonight is the first session with her group. She has been stuck with each one of these women in individual therapy and feels as though the dynamics of the three together could really push them forward. She is all too aware that three does not make a group—it typically just makes trouble—but she feels as though she had to try something, and throwing a fourth member in just to make it a group by therapy standards would do more harm than good. She knows this is going to be a lot of work for her, and she will need to be focused beyond normal. Not an easy task on this particular Wednesday. All day she has found herself drifting off, just thinking about the fabulous date she went on with Greg. It was so fun, so easy; and he is so handsome. She looks at the clock; it's 5:35. *OK, five minutes to lose yourself in your thoughts, and then focus.* She can't help but smile as she leans back into her ergonomic desk chair. He was, hands down, the best kisser she has ever kissed. She closes her eyes and thinks of their good-night kiss. She thinks about how he gently placed both hands on her face and lightly kissed her lips. Her smile grows bigger as she remembers opening her eyes as he pulled away, his hands still holding her face. He didn't say anything; he just looked into her eyes and smiled and then gave her the most amazing open-mouth kiss. Jackie lets out a sigh, and she leans her chair forward and thinks, *Great, now I'm just turned on. OK, focus!*

Shelly walks into her therapist's waiting room. It is actually quite full; one man is sitting in the corner, flipping through his blackberry; an older woman is seated next to him, knitting; and one other woman, looking about Shelly's age, is sitting in the corner, reading a magazine. She looks up at Shelly and smiles, and then looks back to her magazine. Shelly is thinking this woman might be a group member, but one ever knows, as there are other therapists who share the same waiting room. Shelly looks over to the switch box where people go to let their therapist know they are there, and she notices the switch is flipped. She now knows the woman reading the magazine is definitely a group member. *How awkward*, she thinks to herself as she grabs a seat in the opposite corner. About two minutes later, as Shelly is getting more anxious for the session to begin, the door opens, and Shelly looks up to see the most beautiful woman. She stands about five foot ten, although she is wearing high-heeled boots which made her look six feet tall. She has gorgeous long, thick black hair and huge brown eyes. Shelly thinks she might be Spanish. She is impeccably perfect, and quite honestly, Shelly thinks she looks like she should be in Hollywood, not Boston. Even the gentleman who barely took his eyes off of his blackberry is flitting his eyes from his blackberry to this woman, clearing his throat, and shifting around in his seat. Shelly laughs to herself; beauty, albeit fleeting, is powerful. The beautiful woman barely glances around the room before she sits down next to Shelly, crosses her legs away from her, rests her chin on her hands, and stares at the exit door, almost as if she is contemplating an escape.

At 5:55 p.m., Jackie sees the light on her phone blinking, which lets her know her clients have arrived. Jackie heads out to the waiting room and is relieved to see that all three of her female clients have actually arrived. She smiles at all of them. "Ladies."

Shelly, Lauren, and Eva all stand up at the same time, giving each other half-smiles, and follow Jackie back to her office. Jackie's stomach is in knots as she asks everyone to have a seat. She knows she is taking a huge risk by only have three members in this group, and she feels as though she is onstage, not in a therapeutic environment. Of course, she reminds herself, she is also probably picking up on the tension and nerves the three other women are experiencing themselves. Jackie sits down after all have been seated and begins.

"Well, first, thanks to all of you for coming. I know you may be a bit apprehensive, but I would not have asked any of you to be here if I had not thought it would be to your benefit. I know I have spoken to each of you individually about this group and the process; however, I do have some things I want to go over first. And before I even do that, if we could just introduce ourselves—and at this point, just your first name is fine." The ladies introduce themselves in all of five seconds flat.

"OK," Jackie continues, "hopefully this is the most talking I will be doing. I do want to go over some general rules that I would like everyone to agree to. Additionally, when I have finished, if any of you have any other rules you would like to add, please do so." Jackie looks over her left shoulder to the easel she has placed outside the circle of furniture. On the easel is a large white pad of paper that lists the group rules, covering everything including confidentiality, abuse, reporting mandates, respect, and the last one she slipped in: "No exchange of money, goods, or services while in this group."

The ladies all agree to the rules, but all are curious about the last rule.

"Yes, well, at this moment, this rule might not make sense to you, but trust me, it will later," Jackie tells them.

They all agree; however, the last one makes Eva feel a bit uncomfortable. Eva is curious as to who would possibly exchange anything with people they don't know and with whom they are in therapy. She is very conscious of the fact that she has a great deal of money and is in a powerful corporate position. She has, over the years, been approached by distant family or even faint business acquaintances looking for a loan or seed money. Eva looks at the other women, who appear quite put together, nicely dressed, and attractive. She wonders if Jackie may have written this rule for her, to avoid solicitation; and she is now a bit wary of what exactly she has gotten herself into.

"Great." Jackie says, happy all are satisfied with the rules at hand. "Now, I asked each of you in our last individual sessions to answer a question and bring it to the group today. I asked you all the same two questions. What would you do if you only had six months to live? And what would you regret if you had already lived your six months? Did you all complete it?"

The women reach into their purses and bags and pull out their notebooks with the homework Jackie had asked them to complete.

"Great. OK, now I want you all to rip it up."

The women look at Jackie in shock.

"What?" demands Eva.

"Rip it up," repeats Jackie.

"But Jackie, I spent two weeks stressing about this," Lauren states, annoyed. She makes eye contact with the other women.

"OK." Jackie holds up her hand to the protests and eye rolls. "Look, if what you have written is more than fifty percent true and real, then you don't have to rip up your work."

Jackie makes eye contact with each woman, one by one. Eva finally just rolls her eyes and rips up her paper. Lauren quickly follows suit and, while ripping, adds, "Oh, thank God."

Shelly hangs her head; then she laughs, raises her head, and starts to rip. "Truly, when I was writing this at five o'clock, I thought twenty percent true was good enough."

The women all exchange laughs and smiling glances. Jackie sits back, completely relieved that this exercise did not backfire on her. They start to commiserate on how much time they spent thinking about the question, the stress, the fear of presenting in front of all these other people they do not know. They share similar feelings about the process and a similar process toward the exercise. Jackie jumps in on a few occasions to point out similar qualities the women all share, which then catapults them into more stories about worry, fear, anxiety, and so on, usually all for nothing. The women expertly, yet unknowingly, guide the "get to know you" process through this one, shared experience. They open up on a superficial level, demonstrating shared reactions to similar situations. Jackie lets the group go in the direction it wants, only interjecting when she feels they have hit on a major point or the group needs some prompting to continue the free flow of conversation. It is exactly what Jackie wanted this first group to be: a planned process, yet spontaneous enough for the women to have an unrestrained conversation and begin to bond in a very nonthreatening way. The women bond over everything from their ages, to being (for the most part) single in such a young city, to even the minor expression of isolation they at times feel. Granted, it is all very surface stuff, but that is all it needs to be. They just need to get to know each other a little bit and to feel a bit more relaxed. As the clock nears 6:55 p.m., Jackie begins to wrap things up. She thanks everyone for being willing and active participants and hopes that everyone will agree to another session next week; however, the next session will be an hour and a half. The women agreed without hesitation and are still chatting as they put on their coats and exit Jackie's office.

Jackie takes a deep breath as she shuts her office door. She is incredibly thankful that the process has worked; however, she knows her biggest tasks lie in front of her. And she only has five more weeks to accomplish them. She is breaking every rule in the book; she only has three members to her group and only six sessions planned. If she were playing the game Bullshit, every therapist in the room would call her out. *Huh,* Jackie thinks to herself. *Bullshit—that is perfect.*

BRIOCHE TECHNOLOGIES HOME OFFICE

John pulls out of the Brioche Technologies parking garage and heads West on Wilshire Boulevard toward Beverly Hills. It is another typical January day in Los Angeles: bright sunshine, dry air, and seventy-two degrees. And although most would say the California lifestyle is much more laid back than that of the East Coast, the warm air and palm trees are not taking away any of John's anxiety right now. He has too many investors asking too many questions. Two in particular are making John a bit nervous. John pulls out his phone and dials Katz's cell number.

"John, what can I do for you?" answers Katz.

"Katz, my friend, where are you?" asks John.

"I just landed in Chicago. So don't even begin to tell me about the bright sunshine in LA."

"Katz, I need you in Boston."

"Ok." Katz stops walking midway through the terminal, wanting to hear John's request before he goes any further toward exiting the airport. "When and why?"

"Now. I need you to go Boston now, and I need you to keep an eye on Mark and Bill. They have been asking too many questions. Take them out to dinner, find out as much as you can. Just do what you do and calm them down. They need some serious attention right now, and I can't be the one to give it to them."

Katz lets out a huge sigh. He walks over to an empty gate seating area and flops down on a seat. "Do you want to elaborate on what I may be facing?"

"I do, but not now. Go to Boston and call me from your land line, and I will fill you in." John hangs up.

Katz sits back in the gate seat and shakes his head. He sends a text message to his assistant to cancel his Chicago appointments. "Shit!" he mumbles as he punches the seat next to him.

SESSION 2

Jackie scrambles to get her office set up before the second session of her group. She pushes aside her leather chairs and makes room for the card table and four folding chairs she borrowed from a friend. She is grateful she has such a big office space. She drapes the table with a black tablecloth and carefully places a deck of cards in the center of the table. *Perfect*, she thinks and laughs to herself.

As the women enter Jackie's office, they all have perplexed looks on their faces, noticing the card table and chairs in the center of the room.

"What's this?" asks Shelly. "Poker night?"

"I hope not. I am a bad poker player," Lauren quips.

"It is an icebreaker," Jackie replies. "Have a seat."

The ladies unceremoniously, and without conversation, remove their hats and gloves, hang their coats and purses on the backs of the chairs, and sit with their eyes on Jackie.

"OK," Jackie begins. "We are going to begin with a game called 'Bullshit.' Anyone know the game?"

The ladies look at each other and then back at Jackie, all shaking their heads no.

"Well, it is quite simple. The object of the game is to be the first one to get rid of all of your cards. We deal all of the cards, and one person starts. You go in order of number, and aces are low. So, for example, Eva would start, and she would put as many aces down as she has in her hand. Shelly would then have to put down twos, Lauren threes, and myself the fours, and so on. You may not have the number that you are supposed to put down, so you can put another card down or two other cards down. The cards go facedown on the table, so no one knows what you are putting down. If, however, anyone thinks you are lying, they can call bullshit, and you must show the cards you put down. If you were lying, you acquire all of the cards in the pile. If you were not lying, the person who called bullshit acquires all of the cards in the pile. Any questions?" Jackie asks as she looks at each of the women.

"What is the point to this?" Eva demands.

Jackie smiles as she replies, "Let's play, and then you can tell me."

The women cut the cards to see who will deal and go first. Eva has the honor of being dealer and the first. She expertly shuffles the deck and deals the cards like a Vegas poker dealer. The game begins at a slow, calculated pace. As the women become more comfortable with the rules and each other, more "bullshit" is called, and more laughter fills the room. For forty-five minutes, the women play game after game, becoming more daring and more competitive. Eva wins the third round by placing her final card; Shelly calls bullshit to no avail. Eva had the right card, and Shelly now holds so many cards she can barely handle them. At this point Jackie decides the game has been effective and puts end to the cards and begins the work.

"Well, ladies, can anyone answer Eva's original question: what is the point?" Jackie inquires.

Lauren, still giggly from the game, replies, "Yes—that Eva is a really good liar."

Eva smiles but feels her stomach turn; she is a good liar, but she does not want anyone to know that. Jackie notices Eva's expression begin to harden. Jackie resists every urge to jump in and save Eva. Lauren notices that Eva's expression has changed, and, feeling badly, she tries to rectify her previous statement. "I'm sorry, Eva; I did not mean that in a negative way. I should have said you are a good card player."

"It's OK," Eva responds. "You are right; I am really good at hiding things. I have a good poker face."

"Well, clearly, that is not something I have." Shelly enters the conversation. "My question is, how? How do you do it? Do you practice? Is it something you have always been good at? I would like to learn how to do it."

Eva feels her heart begin to pound and her hands becoming clammy. Eva puts a smile across her face and responds, "I think I have learned how to do this through my work. The work can be very stressful and very emotional at times; however, those are the times when you absolutely cannot show any emotion. It would show a weakness or vulnerability to my competitors—or my male colleagues. Not being emotional and mastering the poker face has brought me great success."

It takes everything Lauren has not to call Eva out on her response. Lauren feels as though Eva was lying. Eva's response was effortless, like she had practiced for days. Her face was calm; her hands steady and lightly clasped together resting on the card table. Her voice was smooth, and her delivery was as flawless as the skin on her face.

"Well, then, why are you here?" Lauren asks.

Eva was a bit taken a back and felt her head pull away from the table. She felt angry. It was everything she could do not respond with bitterness and sarcasm.

"I do not know." Eva delivers another emotionless, spotless response. Eva then turns to Shelly and asks, "Why are you here, Shelly?"

Shelly is shocked that the question is directed at her. She begins to shift in her chair. She looks up at the ceiling and then back down at the group. She leans back, collects her long blond hair with both of her hands, raises it up, and then lets it drop around her shoulders. She lets out a big sigh and puts her head down on the table. After what seems like eternity, she picks her head up, looks over at Eva, and says, "You know, I am not really sure. I mean, I am in therapy because

I am unhappy with the way my life is going, and I want it to change. Jackie asked me to join the group because she felt as though I am stuck, and this might be a good thing to push me through." Shelly looks around the room nervously, waiting for a response.

"That's the same thing you said to me, Jackie," Lauren says.

"To me as well," adds Eva.

All eyes are now on Jackie. Jackie sits silent for a minute and then calmly responds, "Does anyone know why I think they are stuck?"

All of the women slowly shake their heads no.

"OK, then let me ask you this: what would keep someone stuck? Generally speaking," Jackie asks.

The women discuss various thoughts, behaviors, and concrete things that may keep people stuck. After some back and forth, they collectively decide that fear is a big thing that keeps people stuck.

"Good." Jackie looks around the room, being sure to make eye contact with each of the women. "Fear is what we all agree on. It is something that can play a significant role in keeping someone stuck, preventing someone from moving forward in his or her life, from changing a behavior or pattern. It is true that I asked each of you to join this group because I thought you were stuck. If fear is a key factor in keeping someone stuck, then I would like each of you to come here next week prepared to discuss your fear."

The silence is deafening. No one moves. No one seems to be breathing. After a few minutes, Lauren asks, "What if we don't know what that is? I mean, if we knew, we would be addressing it."

Jackie lets the silence last a bit longer this time before she responds. The women begin to move in their chairs, clasping and unclasping their hands, and Shelly twists her hair. "Well, I have spoken about fear with each of you individually. One is typically fearful of something—of something being found out or of being vulnerable. People are often fearful of rejection or failure. Perhaps we are fearful of being true or truthful about who we really are or an aspect of our lives; because it would make us vulnerable. I look forward to the discussion next week."

The women stand up. Without a word or a glance at each other, they put on their coats, hats, and gloves; collect their purses; and leave the room, single file. By the time the line of the three women reaches the exit door of the building, each has a cell phone up to her ear. They each speak to or pretend to be listening to someone on the other end of their phone. They give each other a quick, silent head nod, smile, or wave to acknowledge their departure.

KATZ'S APARTMENT

At 8:00 p.m. Katz unlocks his apartment door, throws his keys onto the kitchen counter, and wheels his carry-on into the bedroom. He takes off his suit and throws it into his dry-cleaning bag. He slides into his sweatpants and his favorite Harvard sweatshirt. He doesn't bother to turn on any lights; the view is better with the lights off. He grabs a beer out of his fridge and plops himself on the couch. He reaches over and grabs his portable phone, hesitating before dialing John's number. Does he really want to know what is going to be said?

"Katz," John answers the phone after one ring.

"Hi, John, I just got back from Chicago. What is the plan?"

"Well, I need you to pay a visit to both of the men tomorrow. Arrange a dinner, take them out, and just calm them down. I also need you to find out what they have been up to. Keep an eye on them."

"What do you mean, keep an eye on them?"

"I mean exactly that, Katz. Follow them; see what they are up to. They are smart men who are very worried about losing a lot of money. I am worried they might try to get to Eva. That would be very bad for all of us."

"Um…OK," Katz responds slowly, demonstrating his hesitation and confusion.

"Look, I just need you to keep an eye on them and tell me immediately if they are at all getting involved with Eva. This is important, Katz. They can't communicate with her. That could blow the whole operation. You're still dating her therapist, right?"

"Yes."

"Any new information from her?"

"No, but I'm still working it."

"Good. Just a few more weeks, Katz, and we will be home free."

"All right, I will let you know how it goes with the boys. But what if they do get to Eva?"

"I have a plan for that, Katz. Just let me know if they do." John hangs up.

Katz puts down the phone and stares blankly at all of the lights in front of him. The bustling Boston financial district is now barely a buzz. Katz chose this location many years ago. He wanted to live and breathe the core of the city. Unfortunately, this part of town seems to die down once the clock strikes 6:00 p.m. People work here, but they do not remain here. The evening work keeps happening, but in other neighborhoods: the Back Bay, Beacon Hill, the North End—everywhere but downtown. Katz continues to stare into the office windows that are still lit. He notices a person moving around in the State Street building. He looks like a younger man, middle floor, probably a midlevel manager staying late trying to work his way up the floors. Katz remembers those days, fresh out of business school. He remembers being bright-eyed and eager to climb the corporate ladder, going the extra mile, all to gain the experience to someday be on the top floor, be the coveted CEO. Katz sips his beer, his face expressionless. He has always been well liked. People always seem to gravitate towards him. He was the star quarter back of his high school football team and the valedictorian. He went on to Harvard and graduated with honors. He was pursued by all of the fortune 500 companies. Everyone wanted him on their team. He had a very promising future. He could have done anything…that is, until he did the absolutely wrong thing.

SESSION 3

Lauren, Four Days before Session 3

Maria races up the grand staircase in the lobby of the Boston Park Plaza hotel. Her pace quickens as she nears the doors to the ballroom. She can hear Lauren barking orders as her hand reaches for the brass handle. Maria opens the door to find Lauren, impeccably dressed in a soft gray skirt suit and high black heels, holding a maroon tablecloth in one hand and loudly telling the hotel staff that they have the color all wrong.

Maria runs toward Lauren, calling her name. Lauren turns to Maria, daggers practically shooting from her eyes. She now turns her loud voice and anger toward Maria. "Where the hell have you been? This is a disaster; they have the colors all wrong! I thought you could handle this, Maria!"

Maria does her best to keep her cool. She has only seen Lauren this upset a few times, and usually with good reason. "Lauren," Maria states in her calmest voice, "maroon is the right color. Remember, the bride changed her mind again, back to the maroon."

"What?" Lauren is still angry and looking perplexed.

"Here." Maria pulls out her folder and shows Lauren the last notation, dated and signed by the bride, requesting the maroon tablecloths.

"Ugh," Lauren grunts as she looks at the ceiling and pumps her fists in the air. She takes a deep breath, turns to the hotel staff, and sincerely apologizes. She then turns to Maria and does the same. Lauren quickly turns and heads out of the room across the hall to the bathroom. Maria gives the hotel staff an "I am sorry" look and then quickly follows behind Lauren. Maria enters the bathroom and finds Lauren with both hands on the sink, holding herself up and shaking her head.

"Lauren," Maria says, looking intent and concerned, "what is going on with you? This is not like you. You are the one who always maintains her cool. You are always in control while everyone else, including myself, is flipping out around you."

"I know. I'm sorry, Maria. I'm not sure what has been bothering me this week. But something is. I have a very uneasy, out-of-control sense, and I cannot put my finger on it. Bear with me, Maria, and if you would, take the lead tonight."

Maria nods her head in affirmation. "All right, I am going to go check on things. I can handle this, Lauren, I promise."

"I know you can, Maria; thank you."

Maria leaves the room, and Lauren closes her eyes and takes some long deep breaths to calm herself down. She pulls her cellphone out of her suit pocket and dials her therapist. Relieved to hear the voice mail pick up, Lauren waits for the beep: "Hi, Jackie, this is Lauren. Listen, I am sorry, but I am not going to make the group session this week. I have a difficult wedding coming up, and the parents are insisting I meet them while they are in town. And, well, of course, they are only in town *Tuesday* evening. My apologies to Eva and Shelly."

Twelve Hours before Session 3
Eva reaches for her alarm clock at 5:59 a.m. and shuts it off one minute before it is set to go off, just as she does every morning. She swings her legs out of the bed and onto the floor; sitting at the edge of her bed, she reaches her hands to the ceiling for a long stretch. She walks into her bathroom and smiles as she looks around. She loves

her redesigned bathroom. She attempted to take the best things she had seen from her countless hotel stays and incorporate them into her perfect bath. Her floors are a crisp, white heated tile, and her walls are painted a soft gray. To her left are her heated towel racks, and on a hook hangs her white terry cloth robe. On the other side of the towel racks is the most magnificent shower with a half-glass front. The shower contains ten different showerheads and a hand-held massaging head. In the corner of the shower is a long bench for sitting and shaving. Her shower is big enough to hold four people, but it holds just one. To the right, just in front of her shower on the opposite wall, is a nine-drawer marble-topped vanity with two brushed-nickel sinks sitting on top. A mirror hangs over each sink, and light fixtures are between the mirrors. The vanity continues and drops down a foot. Another mirror and a high-back chair draped in white constitute her makeup area. Just next to the makeup area, a flat screen TV is mounted in the corner. As you turn the corner, you see a large soaking tub with shelves on the sides for candles and one large enough to hold a book. The tub sits perfectly across from the mounted TV. Still further back you see a door, which leads to the toilet area, tucked away privately. The mix of whites and grays creates a soothing atmosphere. Lighting is built into the ceiling and the walls. Perfectly selected black-and-white landscapes decorate the walls, and music is accessible in every room of Eva's penthouse.

 Eva brushes her teeth and washes her face. She gathers her long, thick black hair and ties it in a low ponytail. She leaves her bathroom and takes a left into her walk-in closet.

 The closet is twice the size of her childhood bedroom that she shared with two other children. She puts on her running gear, sits down on the cushioned bench in her closet, and ties her running shoes. She walks back into her bedroom, reaches for her cell phone on her bedside table, and leaves a voice mail for her therapist, stating that she will not be attending the session tonight as she has a meeting she must attend. She grabs her keys and heads out the door for her morning run.

Two Hours before Session 3

It is four o'clock on Wednesday afternoon. Shelly sits on her shag rug in her living room. Papers, bills, a calculator, and a notepad surround her. She pounds away at the calculator keys, adding up a long string of numbers she has written down. Her calculator spits out a number; she clears it and adds all of the numbers again. Her calculator gives her the same number; she decides to hit clear and do it one more time. Again, her calculator gives her the same number. Her hands begin to shake; she writes down the number at the bottom of the column of numbers and circles it. She cannot believe her eyes. She leans back against her couch. Suddenly, Shelly springs to her feet, runs to the bathroom, hangs her head over the toilet, and throws up. Still on her feet, she flushes the toilet and slides over to the sink. She braces herself with one hand on the sink, turns on the faucet, and rinses her mouth. She grabs her toothbrush and toothpaste, and brushes her teeth slowly. She splashes water on her face and looks into the mirror. She stares at her reflection. Her unwashed hair is pulled back into a ponytail. Her skin is pale, almost gray from the sunless winter months. Her eyes are glassy, and her face is expressionless. She just stares at herself, horrified.

Shelly eventually stops staring. Like a robot, she leaves the bathroom, grabs her cell phone off the kitchen counter, walks six steps, and slumps back down on her living room floor, leaning against her couch. She looks at her phone, inhales, and slowly lets out a deep breath. She composes a new text message to her therapist:

Jackie, I am sorry, but I will not be at group tonight. A stomach bug just came over me, and I am really sick.

6:00 p.m. Wednesday: The Start Time of Session 3

Jackie sits in her office, rocking back and forth in her mesh ergonomic chair, feeling defeated. Crushed, actually. She spins around and rests her elbows on her desk, covers her face with her hands, and lets out a muffled, drawn-out "Ugghhhh." Jackie is completely frustrated. Her biggest fear is coming true. She knows she pushed them too hard, too fast. That was the risk of this group. They are all very stuck and have been for quite some time. She also has a short time frame with which to work with everyone. The bond between them is not strong enough for all of them to take such a risk in front of the group. She tries calling her supervisor; however, Janice is unavailable. Jackie knows she will get a return call, but she is concerned about the timing. She does not want to lose everyone permanently or lose the momentum. She needs to act fast. She needs to fix this, but how?

Jackie lets out another big sigh and decides to move. She has been in her office since eight o'clock this morning; she thinks that if she can change the scenery, perhaps she will have some brilliant idea. *A miracle*, she thinks to herself. *I need a friggin' miracle.* Jackie unplugs her laptop and plops it into her bag along with her notebook. She tosses her cell phone into her purse and grabs her coat, hat, and gloves from her office closet. She bundles up, slings the bags over her shoulder, and heads out the door for a chilly walk home. All the while her head is spinning.

Jackie arrives home by 6:40 p.m. to a quiet building. Rick and Tom are away for the week, and her other neighbor keeps to himself. She goes through her usual routine, changes into her favorite pair of jeans and a fleece, and cleans up the coffee and dishes from the morning. She does not feel like eating, so she pours a glass of red wine, throws on her down jacket, and heads upstairs to the deck to smoke a cigarette. Jackie takes a drag of her cigarette, lifting her head to the sky as she slowly exhales. She looks at the magnificent view, which she never tires of. She is looking for inspiration, an answer, somewhere among the building lights, in the drags of her cigarette, in the sips of her wine, somewhere…she is hoping to find an answer to her situation. She doesn't.

By 8:00 p.m., Shelly has managed to take a shower, blow-dry her hair, apply make-up, and put on her best straight-out-of-work outfit. A tight black skirt that stops just below her knees; a fabulous $200 white blouse with perfect detail along the collar and sleeves;

and her insanely expensive, high, spikey, black leather boots. She pulls her last-resort, for-emergencies-only visa card out of her drawer and carefully places it in her wallet. She puts on her black cashmere coat, a fabulous black cashmere scarf, and black leather gloves. She leaves her building, hails a cab a block away at the corner of Mass Ave and Beacon Street, and instructs the cab driver to head to the Four Seasons. *At least I can pretend I am rich*, Shelly thinks to herself.

The doorman at the Four Seasons greets her with a smile and a "Good Evening" as he opened the door to the hotel. She quickly turns left as if she has done this a thousand times, passes the grand staircase, and heads into the bar. Shelly scans the seating area, which is scattered with a few couples and one group of gentlemen; she passes them by, her eyes fixed on the dark mahogany bar. *Slim crowd*, she thinks to herself. She pulls out a bar stools as she sheds her coat, noticing a few potentials are looking her way. She sends one rather handsome, slightly gray-haired gentleman a quick bat of her eyes and then turns her attention to the bartender. The bartender comes over to Shelly with a freshly poured bowl of mixed nuts and asks, "What can I get you, miss?"

"Vodka martini, extra olives, please," Shelly replies.

"Put that on my tab, Dan," a deep voice states from behind Shelly.

Shelly turns to see the rather handsome, slightly gray-haired gentleman standing behind her to the left. "Oh, please, you do not have to do that," Shelly half-heartedly protests.

"I insist," the gentleman replies. "May I?" He points to the barstool next to Shelly.

"Of course, and thank you."

"Bill," the gentleman states and holds out his hand. *How ironic, I seem to be haunted by Bills these days*, Shelly thinks to herself as she extends her hand to introduce herself.

"Shelly."

"Shelly," Bill says and then holds a dramatic pause as he looks at her inquisitively. "You look more like a Heather or Tiffany."

Shelly wants to roll her eyes. *Oh boy,* she thinks to herself, *he is one of those. One of those arrogant, 'I am going to try and charm you with my not so charming wit' guys. He is the guy who believes if he comes off egotistical and a bit condescending, then I will be attracted to him like a bee is to honey.* Shelly actually thinks he could be the guy who would use the bee-to-honey line. "Well, sorry to disappoint; my name is Shelly."

"Oh, Shelly, no, you have a great name; you are not disappointing anyone. Why would you think that? I was just simply pointing out that Heather or Tiffany seem to be more in line with your look. The blond hair, the impeccable dress, and beautiful figure—you remind me of an actress…"

As Bill was talking, Shelly could not help but feel as though she has seen this man before. He is unfamiliar, yet something is familiar; she is just unsure of why. At that moment Bill is distracted, as with many other pairs of eyes that were at the bar. Shelly turns to see what all of the eyes were looking at. *Shit,* Shelly thinks to herself.

Eva walks into the bar at the Four Seasons, fresh off a twelve-hour workday. She strolls by the couples and gentlemen seated in the lounge area of the bar, ignoring the long stares; her eyes stay focused on the bar. As she comes up to the bar, she is shocked to see Shelly, who is looking fabulous, chatting with an older gentleman. *Shit,* Eva thinks to herself, and at that moment, Shelly turns and makes unexpected eye contact with Eva.

Eva quickly assesses the look on Shelly's face; and without thinking, Eva throws her arms up in the air, smiles, and greets Shelly with, "Love, I am so sorry I'm late. It is so good to see you. Have you been waiting long?"

Shelly stands up and accepts Eva's extended arms. With a sheepish grin she replies, "No, not long at all; so great to see you."

Eva instantly takes control of the situation. "Good, let's go grab a seat over there and start catching up." Eva waves to the bartender, "She will have a fresh drink, and I will have a scotch on the rocks. We will be over there." Eva points to an open spot with a table and four high-back chairs.

"I will bring them right over," the bartender replies.

"But, Eva, I have barely touched this drink," Shelly protests.

"Love, please, leave it. Let's start with fresh drinks together; it has been way too long."

As Eva is beginning to pull Shelly toward the table, the older gentleman interrupts, "Well, would you two beautiful ladies like some company?"

It takes everything Eva has to not go off on the creepy older man. She just looks him dead in the eye and says, "No." She then helps Shelly gather her coat and purse and walk over to their new spot. As Eva and Shelly walk over to their new table, they are both shocked as they almost literally run into Lauren.

Lauren's eyes widen as she sees Eva and Shelly standing in front of her. She is confused on so many levels, but without time to think of anything clever, she utters, "Um, hi!"

Shelly cannot believe how poorly her night is going, and this tops it off. "Hi, Lauren, care to join us?"

The ladies are quiet as they sit down in the high-back chairs circling a square cocktail table. The bartender brings over the drinks for Eva and Shelly, and he shines a big, comfortable grin when he sees Lauren.

"Hi, Dan, how are things tonight?" Lauren asks.

"Not bad, Lauren; the usual?"

"You know it. Thank you Dan."

The women speak a little about how cold it is outside. Mostly they sit in an uncomfortable silence, making little eye contact with one another, waiting for Lauren's drink to arrive.

"So, Lauren, how do you know the bartender so well? He is cute," Shelly inquires, rather provocatively.

Lauren laughs. "Ha, not what you're thinking! I do a lot of weddings here, so I know most of the employees."

Dan arrives quickly with a vodka on the rocks and a bowl of mixed nuts. Eva expertly hands Dan her credit card and asks that he keep the tab open. Lauren and Shelly both protest, but Eva waves them off. Eva raises her glass. "Cheers," she says, and Lauren and Shelly follow suit.

"Thank you, Eva, for saving me," Shelly says sheepishly.

"Anytime."

"Saving you?" Lauren questions.

"Yes, I was at the bar, and that older gentleman practically had a drink in front of me before I even sat down."

"Ah, I see," Lauren responds as she looks over toward the bar. "Which one?"

Shelly looks to the seats they were sitting in, and the gentleman is gone. There is some money left on the bar. She takes another scan of the bar and the lounge. "He's gone." Just as the words come out of her mouth, a chill runs down her spine.

Lauren notices Shelly's quick shiver. "Are you OK?"

"Oh, yes, fine. I am glad he has disappeared."

"Just as well; he was a fake," Eva adds.

Both Shelly and Lauren look at Eva confused.

Eva explains, "He is a pretender. He is good-looking enough, but he is pretending to be something he is not. You could tell; there was something off about him. He was trying too hard."

"You know, Eva, that's true. He was rambling on about my name and that it did not seem to fit me. He seemed uncomfortable. You barely spoke to him, but you're right."

"Wow, Eva, you are good!" Lauren states.

"It's my thing. I am in a great number of hotel bars, and it is a game I play, watching, observing, seeing if I can guess a person's story."

"Let's play it!" Shelly says excitedly.

"OK," says Eva, slightly amused by the naïveté of the women she is with. She looks around the room. "The group of gentlemen enjoying their Scotch: what do you think?"

"Hmmm," Shelly ponders. "Local politicians or lawyers?"

"I agree," Lauren adds.

"No," Eva says. "Look at the floor next to the younger man. He has a large satchel with his brochures sloppily hanging out. He is selling…probably a higher-end medical device. I am guessing those gentlemen with him are surgeons."

"You are good," Lauren says. "How about those two couples?"

Eva observes the two couples for a few seconds and begins, "They live in the suburbs. They probably have kids at home, which is why they are having a nightcap at eight thirty in the evening. Most city couples would just be figuring out what they want to eat at eight thirty at night. There is a comfort among them, so they know each other well. But husband A, the blond guy, is detached and seems uncomfortable. He is trying to slouch and look relaxed, but he is constantly looking around. The others all seem at ease. Except you can notice wife B, the redhead, shoots him some interesting glances. Oh, ladies, I think we are witnessing a little sexual tension, if not an affair."

Lauren and Shelly observe the couples for a while, and both see the glances between husband A and wife B. "Oh, my God, Eva, you are totally right!" exclaims Lauren.

"OK," Shelly says, "how about the older gentleman at the bar?"

"Well," Eva replies as she studies him carefully, "he is very comfortable here. His attire is tired but of excellent quality. I would guess if he is not of old money, he has had his money for quite some time. He is, however, probably widowed. He is wearing a wedding ring, but every once in a while, he glances down at it and rubs it. And you can see in his eyes that he is sad; he is missing someone."

"God, Eva, I am going to cry!" Shelly proclaims.

Eva gives Shelly an empathetic smile. "Excuse me, ladies. I just need to run to the restroom."

Eva gets up and swings by the bar on her way to the restroom to order another round for the girls. As Shelly and Lauren await Eva's return, they begin to apologize to one another for not attending the group session tonight. They sit and fret about whether or not Eva was the only one who may have shown up. Dan the bartender arrives with a fresh round of drinks.

"Dan," Lauren says with a serious tone, "will you please put these drinks on my account?"

"I am sorry, Lauren, but I can't do that."

"What do you mean, you can't do that? Dan, how much business do I bring into this hotel?" Lauren exclaims indignantly.

"Lauren, you bring in a ton; and normally I would, but Eva—she brings in a huge amount of business from all over the world. She hosts functions here, dinners, and puts people up for weeks at a time. And that is just here in Boston, not to mention the business she and her company do with us globally. Forgive me, Lauren, and please understand, I just can't." Dan makes his statement while nervously looking over his shoulder to be sure Eva is not approaching the table.

"I get it; that is cool. Thanks, Dan," Lauren remarks.

"Thanks for understanding!" Dan picks up the empty glasses and returns to his bar.

Shelly and Lauren just look at each other, each knowing what the other is thinking and how the plot thickens around their mystery group member. Eva gracefully walks back to the table. Both Shelly and Lauren are quite aware of two things. Every single person in the room, man or woman, is eyeing Eva—the men in the room with pure admiration or lust, the women with pure admiration or jealousy. And Eva does not notice, or does not appear to notice, any of it. Eva takes her seat at the table and notices the drinks and the funny looks she is getting from Shelly and Lauren. "Is it OK that I ordered us another round?" Eva inquires.

It takes a second for both Shelly and Lauren to snap out of their heads, and both ladies quickly agree that is wonderful to have a second round and thank Eva to excess.

"What happened while I was in the bathroom? you both seem rather spellbound."

Both Shelly and Lauren inhale deeply. Lauren begins to speak, "Well, Eva…"

Shelly holds up her hand and interrupts Lauren, "I am sorry, Lauren, and I have a feeling I know what you are going to say. However, before we discuss your topic…" Shelly looks at Eva and leans into the table, "Eva, may we first discuss how you walk through a room, and every time all eyes are on you, and it is as if, you do not even realize it? I mean, Eva, with all due respect, do you know what you do to people?"

Eva can feel her heart start to beat faster, and her palms begin to moisten all because of Shelly's last words. Eva shakes her head, and in a bit of a condescending manner, she replies, "Shelly, looks are not everything."

Shelly is all too aware that she has hit a button with Eva. However, against her desire to keep pushing, she decides to just sit back and let Lauren take over.

"Eva, there is an elephant in the room. Shelly and I were speaking when you were in the bathroom. Neither one of us attended this evening's session, and we think we owe you an apology."

Eva, feeling grateful that Shelly did not press the issue of her physical appearance, picks up her drink and takes a slow sip. Calculatingly, she puts it down, looks both girls in the eyes, and replies, "No need; neither did I."

With a sigh of relief from both Shelly and Lauren, Shelly picks up her drink for a toast, "Cheers to that!"

The ladies toast and have a laugh discussing the "excuses" they came up with for not attending and the irony of all of them ending up at the same bar.

"OK," Shelly says, "before we leave, we need to figure out how we are going to address this with Jackie. I mean I, for one, really like Jackie and feel as though she is a very good therapist for me. I want to return to the group, but we have broken a rule by hanging out tonight."

Both Lauren and Eva nod silently in agreement.

After a few moments of pondering, Eva breaks the silence. "If I may," she hesitates, looking to Shelly and Lauren and getting positive nods from both ladies, "we did not intentionally break a rule. It just so happens that I walked into the bar and saw Shelly. We did not plan to meet here. I do not have either of your numbers. And, if it were not for the look of complete shock on Shelly's face quickly switching to an expression of 'please help me,' I would have simply given you a hello nod and kept to myself. And then, when you walked in alone, Lauren, to see both Shelly and me walking to a table together, what else could we do?" Eva continues, "I live right around the corner; when I am in town, this is where I come."

"I live in the Back Bay as well," Lauren adds. "I do a lot of weddings here; and when I want a quiet place to have a drink, this is where I occasionally come."

Shelly is feeling slightly defensive about Eva thinking she needed to be "saved" from the man at the bar, even though she is the one who first used the "save" term. Shelly never comes here. She can't afford to come here, but she wishes she could. Now she feels defensive and ashamed. *Don't get angry*, she reminds herself. She came here with her head held high, like she belongs, knowing she does not belong here and has absolutely no business being here. She was hoping to make herself feel better, but now she feels worse than when she left her apartment.

"Well," Shelly begins with a hint of anger and sarcasm in her voice, "I never come here. I live in the Back Bay, but bordering Kenmore. I live in a five-hundred-square-foot apartment. My bedroom windows overlook Beacon Street, and last night I was woken up by some college kid throwing up on the sidewalk. I just wanted a change of scenery."

JACKIE

Just before noon on Friday, Jackie is finishing her notes on her last client, and her cell phone starts to buzz. She fumbles through her bag and to try and find it, but to no avail; it stops buzzing. She keeps searching, and when she finally retrieves it, she sees that she has three missed calls from Greg, but no voice mails. *How odd*, Jackie thinks to herself as she quickly calls him back.

"Hi, beautiful!" he says as he answers.

"Hi! Is everything OK?" she asks.

"It is now."

"Seriously, Greg, you called three times."

Greg lets out a big sigh. "Yes, all is well. However, I am not going to make it home in time for dinner tonight. My meetings are running longer than I expected, so I have to catch a later flight home. I am so sorry; I was really looking forward to seeing you. I miss you."

"Oh, of course, no problem. I completely understand. Work comes first."

"Are you sure?" he asks.

"Yes, Greg. Please, it's fine."

"OK; well, I was hoping I could take you to lunch tomorrow. I know this great place by the water. I know it is cold out, but it is supposed to be sunny, and we can enjoy the ocean from inside. Are you free?"

Jackie hesitates for a moment. "Yes, I am free; lunch tomorrow is great."

"OK, perfect. I will pick you up at noon. I can't wait to see you."

"Likewise; safe travels," she says.

Jackie hangs up her phone and lets her head fall onto her desk. She has not seen Greg all week as he has been traveling for work. He has been good about calling and texting while on the road. She understands that travel delays can happen, but to replace dinner with a lunch does not make Jackie feel very confident. Lunch on a Saturday in the dating world means that you are probably going to hear one of a number of things: I really like you, but I am just so busy right now I do not have time to date; or I just don't see this working out; or it's me, not you. Jackie is guessing that she will be hearing the "I am just so busy right now" line.

She has to try to keep her head from spinning about what could have caused this sudden switch from a string of amazing dinner dates to lunch on Saturday. Maybe it is what did not happen. Sex. She brushes it off; she can't control other people's thoughts or behaviors. She says this to her clients all of the time. Sometimes things just do not work out. Though it is much easier to say it to her clients than actually having to go through it herself. She has to force the negative thoughts out of her head; she still has more clients to see.

Jackie pushes her chair back from her desk, puts both feet flat on the floor, and begins to inhale and exhale slowly and methodically. She continues her breathing and begins to repeat, "Stop worrying about what you know nothing about and cannot control." After five minutes of trying to repeat her new mantra, Jackie gives up and hopes that her next few clients have something really interesting and complicated to discuss.

SHELLY

Shelly trudges along Beacon Street Friday evening. It has been a really long, emotional week. She has decided to walk home because she needs the air and the exercise and truly does not feel like riding home on an overly packed Friday evening T. She can feel her phone vibrating in her purse. She doesn't even bother to look to see who is calling. She knows who is calling. They have called forty times today. The infamous "blocked call." She had to clear out her voice mail twice today as the messages they leave are lengthy and keep filling up her voice mail. The same people are calling every time, leaving the same aggressive and threatening messages. They have been calling for months, but now it is getting worse. They are calling more frequently, and their messages are getting more threatening. Today was the worst; they threatened to call her employer. They can't call her employer—they absolutely cannot. She will lose her job, and then what? Everyone loses. They will never get their money, and she will end up homeless somewhere.

Shelly stops at the light at Beacon and Berkley Streets. She watches the long, never-ending stream of cars try to inch their way across Beacon Street onto an already jam-packed Storrow Drive. The amount of traffic in and around Boston never ceases to amaze Shelly. She thinks it must take people hours to get into the city and then hours to get home. She wonders how they have the stamina to deal with the traffic day in and day out. She can't imagine spending so much of her life in traffic; no wonder there is so much road rage.

When the walk sign turns, Shelly weaves between a few cars that did not quite make the light. She needs a solution. She needs something. She wonders if she could reason with the debt collectors; would they listen to her? Would they understand why they absolutely can't call her employer? Should she try? She wishes she wasn't alone in this. She wishes she had someone to talk to. She is walking among hundreds of people and even more sit alongside her, idling in their cars. She doesn't know any of them, not a one. Even if she did, what would it matter? How could they help? Why would they help? This mess is of her own making; it is hers to try and clean up.

EVA

Eva is surprised when she looks at the clock and realizes it is already 8:00 p.m. She has spent the last six hours poring over monthly budget numbers, expenditures, investment income, and projections from Brioche Technologies. Nothing is making sense. One month may have the investment income deposited, and the next month the income is gone; then it appears again, two months later, reported for two months; then it is gone again without the expenditure receipts to explain it. This happens repeatedly, over years, with small amounts, 15,000 to $25,000 at a time, showing up and then disappearing, showing up and disappearing.

She has a list of investors and their projected investment numbers from three years earlier. The projections are $50 million dollars less than the actual listed investments this past spring. It is not uncommon for projections to be off, but John is rarely off, and never by $50 million. And it isn't as though a few investors dropped out or significantly reduced their investment. Everyone reduced his or her investment from the original projections. Eva shakes her head; she does not want to believe what she is now almost certain of. As she stares blankly at her computer screen, her phone's buzzing startles her from her trance. She looks over and sees that her iPhone is not lit up, so she fumbles through her purse to find her flip phone.

"Hi," Eva says.

"Hey, you. How are you?"

"Fine. I'm well; what is going on?"

"Liar. Let me guess: are you sitting in your den, poring over numbers?"

Eva can't help but smile, as Tony knows her so well. "Yes, and it is not pretty."

"Do you have any new information for me?" he asks.

"I will by the time you get here," she tells him. "When are you getting here?"

"Well, not until tomorrow; I am stuck here in DC tonight. But I will come to your place straight from the airport in the morning, OK?"

Eva can't help but be disappointed; she is so stressed out, and she needs Tony right now. She needs her friend, her voice of reason. "Yeah, sure; that is totally understandable, Tony. I am just going to do some more digging to see what I can find."

"OK, but E, be careful. I don't want them suspecting you of anything right now, OK?"

"OK; I will be careful. See you tomorrow."

Eva hangs up her phone and turns her focus right back to the computer screen in front of her. She is just about to print the list of investors and their actual investments when Tony's words of warning make her stop. He is right; she does need to be careful. She is quite certain she has stumbled on to something very illegal, but she does not have all of the information, and anything she prints from the Brioche server will be traceable to her. It is best to sit tight until tomorrow.

JACKIE

Just before noon on Saturday, Jackie finds herself pacing around her apartment. She wishes Greg had just called her and broken it off over the phone; why the lunch? It makes things much more uncomfortable to sit through a meal. Maybe she will listen to him and then storm off. She has always felt a hint of jealously when some of her more demonstrative clients have told her stories of just storming off in the middle of the meal. Some had good reason, and some had absolutely no reason. But she has always wondered why, if justified, she could not just storm off. She can't. She cares too much about what everyone else thinks. She could never cause a scene. *Damn it, just once I wish I could cause a scene,* she thinks to herself.

Jackie's phone buzzes, and she sees it is Greg calling. "Hi there," Jackie answers in her fakest pleasant voice.

"Hi; your chariot awaits."

"OK, I will be right down."

Jackie takes one last look at herself in the mirror as she heads out the door. *You can do this,* she thinks to herself. *Whatever it is going to be, you can handle it.*

As Jackie exits her building, she can't help but smile when she sees Greg standing tall on the side walk, looking exceptionally handsome. She notices, behind him, that his car is double-parked with the hazards on. He turns, sees Jackie, and quickly walks up to her. He grabs her in his arms and squeezes her tightly. Jackie's body instantly tenses. She can't let her guard down now; that will just make the news more difficult. Greg releases his embrace and looks into her eyes. "I missed you," he says. And then he gives her a gentle kiss on the lips. He pulls back again.

"Is everything OK?" he asks.

"Yes, of course; why?" Jackie tries to act surprised by his questioning.

"Nothing; you seem a bit tense."

"Oh, I am sorry; just a rough week with clients."

"Well, then, let's get you into the car."

Greg leads Jackie by the hand and opens her door for her. He waits until she is completely inside and closes her door. Once inside, Greg leans over to steal another kiss from Jackie.

"So, I have a great day planned and an even better surprise for tonight."

"Tonight?" Jackie could not help but hide her shock.

Greg's happy expression drops. "Yeah, I mean, unless you have other plans. I'm sorry, Jackie; I shouldn't have assumed you were free. I got ahead of myself. I should have asked you first. Are you free tonight?" Greg was stumbling.

"No. I mean, yes. I am free tonight. But I thought you just wanted to do lunch?"

"Well, yes, I did, but that was because I couldn't wait to see you. It has been a week. I want to start with lunch. I'm sorry. I am being selfish with your time."

"No, Greg, that is wonderful. I am thrilled. Take all of my time. I am such an idiot." Jackie shakes her head and laughs at herself

"What?"

"It's nothing. It is so ridiculous, I am embarrassed to even say."

"Say it," Greg says in his most over-the-top demanding voice, trying to keep the tone light.

"I thought you asked me to lunch so that you could…you know, stop seeing me."

"Oh, my God Jackie, farthest thing from the truth," he exclaims.

"I know; I am sorry," she says. "I am clearly becoming one of my neurotic, overthinking clients. I am totally embarrassed."

Greg laughs, mostly out of relief that Jackie is still into him. "No, no need to be embarrassed. Let's just call this what it is—poor communication, and mostly on my part. Now, if I may be so demanding as to ask for the majority of your day and evening, I promise you, you will not be disappointed."

Jackie just smiles. How can she not smile when she is with Greg? "Well, since I thought this was going to be a breakup lunch, and it's not, I am quite certain I will not be disappointed."

And disappointed Jackie is not. Greg takes her down to Hingham to have lunch at a restaurant on the water. It is a cold winter day, but the sun is shining brightly, and the ocean is calm and beautiful. After lunch they take the longer route back to Boston, riding alongside the ocean, chatting away and discovering that they both hope to retire to a warm beach town someday. Greg brings her back to her place so that she can change for the evening events, dinner, and a surprise. The surprise turns out to be front-and-center tickets to the performance of Jersey Boys. The performance is spectacular. Both Jackie and Greg are so invigorated from the show that they decide to grab a nightcap at the top of the Hub. It is a perfect night to be on top of the Prudential Center. The evening sky is clear, and you can see for miles.

They each order a glass of Cabernet. When the drinks arrive, Jackie proposes a toast. "To an absolutely perfect day and evening—thank you."

"You are welcome," says Greg. "You know, Jackie, I haven't had this much fun and been this relaxed in such a long time. Thank you. But I feel like I've dominated all of the conversation. You're just so easy to talk to, I can't help it. Does that happen to you all of the time? An occupational hazard?"

Jackie laughs. It does happen to her all of the time and does seem to be an occupational hazard. But she does not feel as though Greg has dominated the conversation at all. "It can be a hazard at times, yes. But I do not feel that way about today. It was nice to get to know more about your work and what you do."

"Tell me more about yours, Jackie. I mean, not specifically, but who is your typical client? Why do people come to you?"

"To be honest, most of my clients are a lot like me, actually. Single, professional women. I have a few men and a few couples, but the majority of my clients are women. I tend to work with the 'worried well,' as I call them."

"What?"

Jackie laughs. "I know, not very empathetic of me to say. But my clients are doing well. They are in good mental health…you know, they may have a little anxiety or situational depression, but they are high-functioning, successful, and smart. They do not have major mental health concerns. But they are usually feeling lonely or that they are missing something, which is typically a partner."

"Interesting. So do they ever talk about work stuff? I mean, can you help with that? I think if I were seeing someone, that would be all I would want to talk about."

"Oh, sure. I talk a lot about work with my clients. I mean, really, that is where they spend eighty percent of their time. So, you know, some are happy, and some want to make a change. Some talk about conflicts they are having or fears about losing their jobs. The usual stuff people think about."

Greg leans in, as he is very interested in what Jackie does. "So do they ever talk about affairs at work or illicit things they think might be going on at work? I mean, you must get a ton of dirt."

Jackie laughs; she is amused by Greg's questions. "It is really not that exciting, Greg. Yes, of course, affairs come up quite a bit. But that is about as criminal as things get."

Greg sits back and lets out a big laugh. He takes a sip of his wine. "But what would you do, I mean, if someone were to talk about things that were illegal? I mean, could you do anything?"

"I think you have been reading one too many crime novels. My clients' lives are not that complicated."

"Cheers to uncomplicated lives!" Greg raises his glass to Jackie. He sits back and just looks at her.

"What?" she asks.

"Nothing. You're just beautiful and wonderful. Listen, I know I travel a lot. And it is hard to date someone who travels all of the time. We can't see much of each other during the week, and it is not like dating someone who works nine to five and is home every night. But I really like you, Jackie. I would like to see where this leads."

Jackie smiles. She can feel a warm rush run through her body. "I would like that, too."

"Well, how about you and I head to Vermont next weekend?" asks Greg. "We can take off on Friday and just spend three days at some country inn."

"Really? That would be fantastic!" she exclaims.

"Could you do it? Could you leave on Friday midday?"

"I will make it work!"

Greg pulls Jackie's chair next to his. He puts on hand on her face and gently presses his lips to hers. He then pulls her closer and slides his tongue into her mouth. Jackie feels as though the room and everyone in it have disappeared. It is just she and Greg. Her heart races, and a rush of desire floods her body. She knows one thing—Vermont is going to be amazing!

SESSION 4

"Jackie, before you start, we—Eva, Shelly, and I—owe you an apology."

Jackie, thinking this should be interesting, just leans back with a surprised look on her face.

"We all," Lauren pauses, "blew you off last week. And we are truly sorry."

"Hmmm," Jackie replies with her head slightly tilted. "Care to elaborate?"

Shelly, Lauren, and Eva just look at each other." No," states Shelly. "We are just sorry."

"Well, let me help," Jackie begins. "Why do the three of you have one apology when you each called me separately? And since you are not supposed to communicate when not in group, I am confused by the group apology."

The women just look at each other with expressions of defeat; they all knew they needed to come clean.

Lauren, wanting to get this over with and feeling an extra sense of obligation to clear the air, begins the explanation. "Well, Jackie, honestly, we did all call you separately, and not knowing about anyone else; however, we all accidentally, and I stress *accidentally*, ran into each other at the same bar. It is hard to avoid the obvious. And we all sat down together, initially not knowing that we had each called in to cancel."

Jackie waited for a moment, sitting with the silence as the other women just nodded their heads in agreement with Lauren's account. "OK," Jackie says after a moment. "Well, we are all adults here. The group rules are put in place for the protection of your privacy. This is a big city with small neighborhoods; you are bound to run into each other at some point. I have a feeling I know why you all called in, but that is for each of you to decide to discuss. I would welcome that discussion as well as where would you like to go from here. This group should run on your agenda, not mine."

The women sit silently for what feels like hours. The minutes tick by slowly. Each of the women occasionally moves around in her chair or lets out a sigh, but they all spend most of the time looking at the ground. The silence is something Jackie is used to dealing with, although she does not like it. She has decided not to save the group with a question or a comment. Jackie's biggest fear for the group already came true: none of them showed up for session three. However, Jackie constantly reminds herself, they all showed up for session four. *Just sit tight*, she repeats to herself over and over.

The time ticking away feels painful for Shelly. She sits in a brown leather armchair in Jackie's office. She wants to curl up and disappear. She knows she needs to talk about things. She is at a breaking point: she is not sleeping, she is drinking every night, and at this very moment, her heart is pounding so hard she feels as though it could explode right out of her chest. Shelly bends down and rests her forehead on her knees, inhales deeply, and slowly exhales. She closes her eyes as tightly as she can, and her heart just beats faster. Finally she lifts her head and blurts out, "I'm a fake, I'm a failure, and I'm screwed!"

The women quickly look over at Shelly, all stunned by her sudden announcement. Then Lauren, unable to control herself, tries to hide her face as she starts giggling uncontrollably. Jackie looks at Lauren with a head tilt and then over to Shelly. Shelly realizes what she just did and starts laughing, too.

"I am sorry, Shelly," Lauren says, trying to get her sentence out amid her laughter. "I am not laughing at you, just the delivery."

"I know," Shelly replies, still laughing at herself. She is laughing in a way she has not laughed in a long time, from the gut. As quickly as the laughter came on, it shuts off, and she begins to sob. Shelly is now crying in a way she has not for years. Uncontrollable, inconsolable sobs.

Lauren, realizing that Shelly is now completely melting down, jumps to her feet and brings over a box of tissues apologizing profusely for laughing. Shelly reaches for the tissues and gives her a wave, shaking her head no, and continues to cry.

"It is OK, Shelly, cry as much as you need to," Jackie states calmly, and gives the other woman a nod to just let Shelly release.

After what feels like an eternity, Shelly begins to feel herself calm down. She is exhausted, she can feel the puffiness of her eyes, her head is full, and she can hardly breathe through her nose. She takes a few deep breaths, as Jackie has been encouraging her to do. Her eyes are still closed; she does not want to face the people in the room just yet. She is trying not to think about how embarrassed she feels. She is trying not to feel for fear she will throw up or start crying again. She wants to leave; she wants to run; and every bone in her body is telling her to just stand up and walk out the door and never come back. But yet, she is exhausted and feels paralyzed as if her body is glued to the chair. She sits up straight, her eyes still closed, and takes another deep breath, inhaling and exhaling through her mouth.

Jackie takes the same deep breath, silently, her eyes fixated on Shelly. Jackie sits up straight in her chair, her arms resting on each armrest, legs uncrossed, feet on the floor, and her face is open and soft. "Shelly?"

Shelly slowly opens her eyes, purposefully keeping them low and just looking across the room at Jackie's hand resting on the chair.

Shelly's eyes slowly make their way up to look at Jackie, and then once she makes eye contact, she quickly, moves her eyes to the floor. Her body is filled with embarrassment and shame. She does not dare look to her left or right. She can't face the eyes she feels staring at her. Shelly thinks she may have just made a huge mistake. She thinks about the other two women in her group. She thinks about what she just blurted out. How could either of these women relate to her? They are nothing like her. They have everything. She knows she needs help and needs to get this out, but she fears she did it in the wrong place. Shelly feels her anger coming up from inside her. She is starting to feel the ground underneath her. Yes, this is what she needs to do, but not with these people. Shelly feels herself readying to walk out the door. Just walk.

"I get it. I mean I don't get everything, and I do not want to assume. But you said, 'I am fake.' I get that. I have felt like a fake my whole life."

Shelly was lifting herself from her seat ever so slightly when she heard the words. She sat back down and pretended to be shifting in her seat. She can't believe what she just heard and looks over at Eva. Did she just hear these words from Eva, perfect Eva?

Eva looks at Shelly and understands her perplexed look. She gives Shelly a half-smile and shrugs her shoulders, looks Shelly in the eye, and says, "A complete fake."

Eva feels a pang of panic quickly shoot through her. She has said too much. That was the wrong thing to say. The group is going to question her; Shelly will rightly question her. She needs to divert things fast; there is too much at stake—she can't come clean. She needs to lie, and lie quickly. She has to. She glances at Jackie and then glances at the clock. Eva is hoping the five minutes left in the group session will buy her more time, a full week.

Shelly notices the eye exchange between Jackie and Eva and she glances behind her and looks at the clock. A blanket of relief comes over Shelly. Time is up. She can leave.

"Well," Shelly says as she turns back to the group, "I guess time is up."

Jackie nods, "Yes, just about, but Shelly, are you OK?"

"I am, Jackie, honestly. And I apologize to all of you for my meltdown."

Lauren takes a deep breath, "Shelly, I am sorry, truly. I did not mean to laugh, I—"

Shelly interrupts her midsentence. "It's OK, Lauren; I needed that laugh…and, well, I needed that cry too. You did not do anything wrong."

"Are you OK though? I mean really?" Lauren asks while reaching over and putting her hand on Shelly's knee.

Shelly feels more relief as she smiles and nods at Lauren.

Jackie looks over at Eva, who looks as though she has completely left the room. The blank look on Eva's face does not surprise Jackie; she is used to seeing that with Eva. What truly surprised Jackie tonight was Eva's rather empathetic comment to Shelly. That surprised Jackie, and that is what worries Jackie. "Eva, anything you need to say before we go?"

Eva blinks and shakes her head as if to wake herself up, "No, no. I just want to be sure, Shelly, that you are OK."

Shelly nods gratefully to Eva.

"Ok then, this was a heavy ninety minutes, and I look forward to seeing you all next week." And Jackie left it at that—no homework, nothing else to think about, knowing that just showing up next week is more than she can ask at this point.

Jackie follows everyone out to the waiting room as the women quietly put on their coats and hats. She waits for everyone to exit and then locks the waiting room door. She stands in the room for a few minutes, listening for everyone to exit the building; then she walks back into her office and plops down in her chair. She spins her chair back to face her desk, takes a deep breath, and cries.

It takes Jackie a couple of deep breaths to calm herself down. It was a very intense session, and she is not surprised she broke down. She does tend to do that on occasion. These tears, however, were not tears of sadness but more of relief. Jackie is relieved that the women showed up and did some work. Jackie checks her voice mails and her schedule and is more relieved when she realizes she has supervision with Janice scheduled for Thursday evening. She knows she needs the supervision desperately.

EVA

Eva turns the corner after having left Lauren and Shelly and being certain that Shelly was feeling well enough to be on her own. Eva has seen that emotion before, and it is always unsettling to her. She shuffles through her bag with one hand while walking quickly up the street; she feels her iPhone and digs a bit deeper into her purse, finally laying hands on her tiny flip phone. She opens it up, her hands shaking a bit; she presses the number one and send.

"E," a voice answers on the other end.

"Hi, can we meet? The usual place."

"Everything OK?"

"Yes and no. I just need to fill you in on some things," says Eva.

"OK, but not the usual; meet me at D Bar in thirty minutes."

"What? D Bar?" Eva is perplexed by the suggestion.

"Yes. D Bar, and take a cab."

Eva looks up to the night sky and lets out a large sigh. She shoves the flip phone back into her purse and heads to Beacon Street to hail a cab. It never takes Eva long to catch a cab; for that she is grateful, especially on such a cold January night. The cab pulls over, and Eva hops in. Before the cabdriver can even ask, she says, "D Bar, please, Dorchester Ave."

"D Bah it is," the cab driver responds with his thick Boston accent. "I will just jump on Storrow to the highway."

"No," Eva states in a commanding tone, "take Mass Ave to Columbia Road."

"OK, miss, whatevah you say."

The cab driver pulls up in front of D Bar, and Eva dreads walking in. She is always uncomfortable having all eyes on her. And she knows that often, many eyes are on her, but she hates it. She pays the cab driver and glances over at the small crowd of smokers pretending to be busy on their phones but constantly glancing at the cab, waiting to see if anyone who excites them may step out.

Eva steps out of the cab, and the smokers hold their glances for a bit longer than they normally would; and then all eyes quickly dart back down to their phones. Eva laughs to herself, knowing all too well that a straight woman walking into a gay bar is not going to excite anyone. Eva walks in slowly, mentally preparing herself for whatever role Tony may be playing tonight. She knows she needs to play along with whatever he does, and she needs to play her part well. As soon as Eva takes two steps into the bar, she hears a squealing, "Ah, there's my girl." Tony comes running, actually prancing, over to her, still squealing with excitement. Eva, quickly registering Tony's pretend gay man act, puts on a big smile and claps her hands with joy as they meet and air-kiss both cheeks. Tony rubs his hand up and down her arm, professing his love for Eva and how much he has missed her. He quickly grabs her hand and whisks her to a quieter corner of the bar. He orders two Scotches on the rocks and continues to play his part until he pays the tab and the bartender disappears to handle the crowd.

Eva looks Tony up and down, trying to absorb her very straight friend playing the part of a rather flamboyant gay man. He is wearing dark fitted jeans that accentuate his strong legs and butt. He has a tight gray T-shirt tucked into his jeans, showing off his slim waist. The length of the sleeves is just short enough to give her an occasional glimpse of his thick, toned biceps. His perfect Latino skin keeps his face looking young. Tony is a handsome, strong man; gay, straight, or otherwise, people always look twice at Tony.

Tony has always been someone Eva can trust. She has known him since she was a child. They spent time in group homes just down the block from one another and went to the same school. They were both shy kids who kept to themselves and stayed out of trouble. When you grow up in a neighborhood full of drugs and violence, you learn quickly whom you can trust and whom you can't. And even with the ones you think you can trust, you remain skeptical. The phrase "sleeping with one eye open" is a great way to describe their childhoods. Tony and Eva are very smart, very good-looking, and very much determined to get out of the lives they were born into. They became fast friends, but never in a romantic way. Still, Eva always remained cautious.

It was not until one Saturday evening when Eva was about fifteen that her caution of Tony turned to trust. She was walking home late from the Dudley T station after having spent hours walking around the Back Bay, daydreaming about her future life. She had stayed a little too long; she missed the six o'clock number 8 bus out of Kenmore and ended up at her T-stop after dark, something she never did. She took all of the streets that were the most lit on her way home; however, her street was darker than most. As she turned the corner, she knew she was going to have to run as fast as she could to the safety of her group home. Before she even reached the corner, two men jumped out in front of her, wielding knives. The streetlight was shining on her, but they were in the dark. She still shivers as she remembers the smirks on their faces, the looks in their eyes. Eva threw her bag at them and just yelled to them to take it. They pushed it aside and laughed and told her they were not after her bag. The two men started walking toward her; and out of nowhere, one fell to the ground, and then the next one fell, not moving, just groaning. Eva thought she heard her named being called, but she was frozen in fear. Then she felt a hand grab her, and she screamed, and then she heard her name again—a version of her name; she heard, "E, you are OK! It's me; come on, we have to run!"

And run they did, as fast as they could, straight toward Eva's group home, stopping just steps before reaching the door, out of breath. Eva remembers asking Tony if he killed them. He had not. Tony had been studying martial arts for years; he just knocked them out. Eva had asked Tony what he was doing there. He explained that he had gone to her group home to ask about their science homework, and when she had not returned, he knew something was wrong. As Tony always put it, he was just at the right place at the right time. Eva recalls telling Tony that the men could have killed him. She then asked him why he was calling her "E."

Tony responded by saying, "The men would have done worse to you, Eva." Tony knew he had hit them hard, and they were out of it, but he did not want the men to hear Eva's real name. Tony then told Eva that the next day, she was going to the gym with him. He said she needed to learn martial arts. She needed to learn to protect herself. And the next day, Sunday, that is exactly what Eva did. Tony was waiting outside for her at ten o'clock in the morning, and she began two of the most empowering and transformational processes of her life: learning to be in control no matter what and trusting someone completely. Tony has called Eva "E" ever since.

"Earth to E!" says Tony, snapping his fingers in front of Eva's face. "Where did you go?"

Eva, coming to, shakes her head, laughing at Tony's flamboyant gestures. "I am here, just gazing at my surroundings."

"Well, get used to it, girl, because this is our new spot."

Eva understands. She knows she meets Tony wherever he has to be. They both left the old neighborhood many years ago. They both succeeded beyond all expectations, Eva going on to great things in private industry and Tony to the FBI. They always supported each other, quietly, and never lost touch, not even for a week. This is why they are here now. The minute Eva became suspicious, Tony was her first phone call.

"E, talk to me, girl; what is going on?" Tony constantly remains in complete character, which Eva finds trying.

"OK, well, you know that group therapy thing I told you I was in?"

"Mmhmmm, the one you *absolutely* need!"

"Whatever; yes…so this woman had a major breakdown today, major crying, sobbing."

"Wait, wait," Tony holds up his arms, "wait, let me guess. Hmm, the bridal chick or the one who you suspect is having major financial trouble? Hmm, post holidays it could be the bridal chick. I have a fifty-fifty chance, but after the holidays, everyone has a financial meltdown." Tony pauses as if he is deeply thinking, and then he looks up at Eva. "Shelly."

Eva rolls her eyes. "Yes, Shelly; thank you for using her actual name."

"So what is the problem?"

"Well, she had this major meltdown."

"Which you can't handle."

"Which makes me feel badly for someone," Eva corrects Tony. "And, well, right before the meltdown, there was this ten-minute silence in the group and she just blurted out that she was a fake, a failure, and screwed."

"Whoa," Tony says. "Lesbian drama!" He waves off Eva and signals the bartender for another round.

"Tony," Eva says, demanding seriousness with the tone of her voice. "I said out loud that I got it. I understood feeling like a fake."

Tony looks at Eva and instantly understands. She was afraid; she needed to let out her fear among strangers, and she was feeling a false sense of security that many in her position feel, some vague familiarity among strangers, a trust that is based on nothing but the words of a complete stranger. They are words that imply trust but are meaningless; they are masked by some ambiguous rule of confidentiality and are brought to a higher meaning with technical terms like "HIPAA" and "mandated reporter." Neither of these does anything but give someone a false sense of security that whatever they say will not show up on the Internet, or worse, cause them actual physical harm. He is both surprised and not surprised. Eva is such a strong woman, but anyone in her position would crave this release.

"Take a sip of your drink," he says.

"What?" Eva looks at Tony, completely confused.

"Take a big sip of your drink and give me the best good-night kiss that you would give your best gay friend."

Eva does as Tony tells her and wraps her arms around him. He presses his lips to her ears and whispers, "Outside your place, ten in the morning Sunday." He releases her and proclaims, "Oh my love, let me walk you to the door; you never know who will hit on you on the way out." Tony waves to all of his friends as they nod approvingly of his delicious female friend. He shoos them off with grand hand gestures, lots of air kisses, and phrases like "Be right back" and "Don't you move, handsome."

Tony hails Eva a cab, kisses her cheek again, and says, "You heard me right; ten in the morning Sunday, outside your place. Just smile and nod." Eva does just that and gives him a half-smile as the cab pulls away, away from her safest spot in the world, away from Tony.

JACKIE

Jackie sends off her last patient of the day. She is grateful to have an hour before her supervision to get organized, return calls, and review her notes for her supervision with Janice. Supervision is a perfect way to end her rather difficult week. Jackie has had longer days this week because she is taking Friday off. She managed to fit all of her clients into four days, but that meant working until nine o'clock most nights and seeing an average of eight clients per day. She has been reminded this week of why she established her six-client-a-day limit.

The end of January and beginning of February tends to be a very difficult time for many of Jackie's clients. Heck, it is a difficult time for many people in the Northeast, Jackie included. The very cold, short days, lack of sun, and lack of opportunity to get outside and exercise seems to put people in a bad mood. Many suffer from the post holiday blues; and for the singletons and even those in a relationship, the anxiety and pressure of the upcoming Valentine's Day doesn't make anything easier. All of the nonsense just seems to bring people down. And let's not forget the full moon! Yes, it has been a heck of a week. However, Jackie knows it is all worth it. Tomorrow she will get up when she wants, sip her coffee, pack her bags, and head to Vermont for the weekend. An entire two and a half days with Greg in Vermont will be heavenly.

Jackie takes a deep breath and refocuses herself. She can't quite start daydreaming yet; she needs to get things in order, including her own mind-set. She picks up the phone and listens to her voice mails, extremely disappointed to have one from Janice. Apparently Janice's father died unexpectedly, and Janice left a very apologetic voice mail for Jackie while heading to the airport. Janice even included a name and the phone number of one of her colleagues in case Jackie should need anything in her absence. Although Jackie is disappointed, she obviously understands and is as impressed as ever with Janice's consummate professionalism. *Well,* Jackie thinks to herself, *when you can't talk about, walk about.* Exercise can do the body and mind just as much good as supervision. Jackie finishes her return calls, puts away all of her client folders, locks the file cabinet, closes up her laptop, and slips it into her bag, leaving her office in tip-top form. Jackie puts on her coat, scarf, hat, and gloves; throws her bag over her shoulder; shuts off the lights; locks her door; and gives herself a little pep talk about taking the very long route home, no matter how cold. She needs to clear her mind.

SHELLY

Shelly has laid low for a couple of days after her "outburst" in the group. She did not want to go out, see anyone, talk to anyone, or be anyone. She called in sick to work, thankful that the flu was going around and half of her office had already been out sick, making her "sick call" very believable. She sat in her apartment for two days, not really thinking, not at all feeling, just lying on her couch, numb. By Friday evening she has had enough lying around. She broke down in group, she finally broke. She knows she needs help, and that is what she is paying for. She needs to use the group, and she needs to come clean. She needs help. As Shelly stands up with the full intention of getting into the shower, she looks over at her kitchen bar top and sees the piles of bills. She sits back down on the couch, puts her head in her hands, and cries.

Shelly cries for some time. She feels so alone and helpless, with a large amount of debt. She looks over at her kitchen counter, and the mounds of bills and envelopes just stare back at her. Shelly knows she is a smart woman; she can't understand how she let things get so out of control. She wishes she had stopped after she maxed out her first credit card. She wonders why she did not stop. It is all too real now. Shelly gets up, walks over to her counter, and begins to sort through her bills.

JACKIE, SATURDAY MORNING

Jackie heads into her office Saturday morning to finish up a few things. She was too depressed on Friday to bother going in. Greg had called her early in the morning, explaining that he had to stay in California one more day as his company was in the midst of getting FDA approval for its new drug. He was extremely apologetic and sent her the biggest bouquet of flowers. He is returning today, and he and Jackie are going to spend the rest of the weekend together. Jackie is just disappointed. She understands that his work is a bit hectic at the moment. She knows health care and understands the potential of having a drug approved. However, she can't hide the fact that she really wanted to spend the weekend in Vermont with her new guy. The guy she is completely falling for. And for that reason, she has allowed herself one day to just wallow in her pity. However, today is a new day; Greg is on a plane, confirmed; and she will have him all to herself for thirty-six hours.

Jackie walks into her shared waiting room. It's empty, but two of her suitemates are working, as their doors were shut and the sound machines are on. Jackie goes to unlock her office door and is surprised to find that it is already unlocked. She knows she always locks her door. Perhaps the cleaning crew forgot to lock it. She checks her locked file closet, just to be sure, and it is locked and secure. She looks around her office, and everything seems to be in order and in its proper place, which makes her feel more certain about the cleaning crew accidently leaving her office open.

Jackie pulls out her laptop and begins working on e-mails and client notes. Her mind keeps flipping back and forth between what she is doing and her infamous group of three. She is concerned about moving everyone forward with so little time left. She is hoping Eva will actually begin to open up. She saw a glimpse of it on Wednesday. She heard Eva connect with Shelly's comment, but she wonders if all will be lost over a week's time.

After finishing everything she set out to do, Jackie realizes she is starving. It is 1:00 p.m., and she is not seeing Greg until 7:00 p.m. Jackie decides now would be a great time to head out and grab some soup on her way home. She shuts down her laptop and double-checks her locked file cabinet, just to be certain. She puts on her winter gear and slings her bag over her shoulder. She grabs her office doorknob and looks behind it to be sure it is locked, even though she can feel it is locked. Out of the corner of her eye she notices a ripped piece of paper on the floor. She thinks that is odd; even though the cleaning crew may have left her door open, they are very meticulous. She picks up the paper, and it has numbers on it. Jackie can't make out the whole thing, and it is not her handwriting; and the numbers do not seem at all familiar. She shoves the paper into her pocket, hoping it will serve as a reminder to address the unlocked door issue with the cleaning crew.

LAUREN

Maria and Lauren belly up to the bar at Four Seasons after orchestrating another successful wedding event. They both let out big sighs of exhaustion.

Dan, the bartender, comes over and pushes a couple of cocktail napkins in front of them. "Another success, ladies. What will it be?" he asks.

"I will have the usual, Dan, thank you."

"I will do an espresso martini, please," says Maria, suddenly perking up.

"Wow, espresso martini, that's new for you, Maria," Lauren states with an inquisitive look.

"I know. I need the caffeine. My friends want me to join them at this hot new restaurant in the Seaport, but the reservation is not until nine thirty tonight. It is Saturday night, Lauren; what are you going to do with the rest of your evening?"

Lauren chuckles at Maria's question. "I would love to say I have big plans, Maria, but I am forty-two and exhausted. I am going to have a drink with you, go home, slip on my yoga pants, and watch some bad television. As you begin to take the first bite of your meal, I will be fast asleep!"

Dan comes over with their drinks, and the ladies clink their glasses to another great wedding. They begin to do some debriefing on what went well and what could be changed. Maria suddenly gets a text message letting her know that her friends have been able to get an earlier reservation exactly one hour from now. Lauren shoos Maria off to go be with her friends, assuring her they can finish the conversation on Monday. Maria thanks Lauren repeatedly, as she always does, and bounces out of the bar. Lauren grins as she watches Maria literally bounce out of the bar. She is so fond of Maria, and she knows how lucky she is to have such an amazing employee—partner, really. Lauren could not do any of this without Maria. Dan comes over to check on Lauren. Lauren declines another drink and just asks for the tab. As Dan brings her the tab, he asks, "So, how do you know Eva Jackson, Lauren?"

Lauren looks up from the tab, still signing her name. Did she just hear him correctly? "Who?"

"Eva, Eva Jackson, the woman you were here with a few weeks ago." Dan replies as he motions to the table Lauren, Shelly, and Eva had been sitting in the night they all skipped out on therapy.

"Oh." Lauren shakes her head as if nothing odd at all had just happened. "Eva, yes. Lovely woman. I met her through a charity thing, and we just run into each other occasionally."

"Cool," Dan replies. "Have a great night, Lauren."

"You too, Dan, thank you." Lauren exits the hotel trying to remember why the name sounds so familiar. No one had revealed her last name during group. "Eva Jackson, Eva Jackson." Lauren just keeps repeating the name to herself; it sounds so familiar to her, but she can't seem to place it.

EVA, SUNDAY MORNING PICKUP

Eva has not stopped spinning about what happened in group Wednesday night. She wants to continue the group. She wants the support. She wants to open up and tell everyone everything. She likes these women. And she feels like she can help them, too. Honestly, help them. It is a nice feeling, a bit like she belongs to something. She can't remember the last time she felt that way.

At 9:50 a.m., Eva's flip phone buzzes. A text message reads:

Put on your running shoes, see you on the Charles, and do not act surprised.

"Shit," Eva says as she flips off the phone. Here she stands in her kitchen, all dressed, makeup applied, and hair washed; and now she has to go for a run. She wishes Tony would give her more notice on what they are doing. But ultimately, she understands, safety comes first. And then she wonders, slightly amused, what—or whom—the heck Tony will be looking like.

Eva gets into her running gear and heads down to the Charles. Even though it is ten o'clock, it is winter in Boston; and as she gets closer to the river, she is very happy she decided to put on her hat and gloves. As she turns down the pedestrian ramp and on to the Esplanade—one of Boston's most famous walking, running, and biking routes, which majestically runs along the Charles River—she sees Tony. Eva actually has to look away to keep herself from laughing hysterically. There before her is Tony, stretching, one leg on the ground and one resting on the back of a park bench. He is hard to miss, considering he is wearing neon green leggings, a skintight black long-sleeve top, pink gloves, and a pink fleece headband. Tony lifts his head from his stretch, sees Eva walking toward him, and lets out a big, long, high-pitched "Hiiiiyee!"

Eva shakes her head as she walks over to Tony, "The eighties called; they asked for their colors back."

"E, I will have you know, the pink is in support of breast cancer, hellooo."

"And the pants? Are you afraid someone is hunting deer along the Esplanade?"

"Oh, E, there *is* hunting going on. And I plan on being the target!"

Eva just rolls her eyes and starts to jog. Tony quickly follows suit. "OK, Tony, but why the over-the-top act? I mean, I know plenty of gay men, and they are not dressing like you, acting like you, or speaking like you, for that matter."

"True, but the man I am after, E, likes men who look, act, and talk just like me. That man is the only man who matters."

"OK, Tony, but even while we are running, do you have to keep it up?"

"Especially in public, E."

"Then why not just come to my place? Why do we have to be here on a freezing-cold Sunday morning?"

"E!" Tony playfully slaps Eva's arm like he is upset. "You love to run, any time of year; and besides," his voice grows quiet, "I would never put your life in jeopardy."

The remark sends shivers down Eva's spine. She knows what Tony does for a living. She knows he goes deep undercover and deals with dangerous situations. She knows she can never ask questions, and she doesn't. But they both grew up in constant danger. They both worked so hard to leave the danger. She has never understood why Tony willingly puts himself back into danger. She has asked many times and always gets the same answer. He says it is different because it is his choice; he is in control most of the time; and he is doing it to try to protect kids. When he puts it that way, she cannot argue. Tony notices the fear in Eva's eyes, and he feels the need to stop toying with her so much.

"E, I am kidding about the last part. I just really needed a run."

They continue along their run, Tony overtly checking out every hot man he sees and covertly longing for every hot woman. They pass the Museum of Science and bear left to run along the Cambridge side of the Charles. Other runners are becoming fewer and farther between, which gives them an opportunity for a real discussion.

"So, E, what is this Shelly's last name?" he asks.

"I have no idea. Why?" Eva is confused by Tony's question.

"Can you find out?"

"I can try. To be honest, Tony, I am surprised you do not know it."

"Well, I can find out, but I thought I would start with the easy route. Do you think you can find out without it being a big red flag in your little therapy thing?"

"I think so, but why?"

As a rather tall, handsome male runner approaches, Tony quickly busts out his flamboyant personality, and rather loudly, "Why, why, why, why, don't you women just get sick of always asking why? Why confuses things; just go with it."

"He is gone, and he is straight." Eva says sarcastically as the handsome runner speeds by.

"Yeah, he was totally straight—and could not get enough of you, I might add."

"Do I detect a hint of jealousy, Tony?"

"No, pure admiration, E."

"So, back to why," Eva says, not backing down.

"Look, we are at a very sensitive time right now. I do not want anything to blow it. You are telling me that there is a woman who is associated with you who has financial problems. I want to know who she is and keep an eye on her, that's all."

"Tony, she is harmless."

"Well, that may be, E. Lots of people are harmless, but desperate people can quickly turn less harmless. This is what I do, E; let me do it. And on second thought, *I* will find out her last name. I do not want you to raise any eyebrows. Where did you say she lives?"

"You are making her out to be some sort of criminal, Tony. She is harmless."

"E," Tony says firmly.

"She lives in the Back Bay somewhere. She said closer to Kenmore, I think."

Tony grins at Eva as they make their way closer to the Mass Ave bridge. He points across the Charles River to the Back Bay, swirling his finger in the air as if he is drawing a circle around the buildings, squints his eyes as though he is very serious, and says, "So, somewhere right about there?"

"Whatever, Tony. Can we just speed up the pace as we run over the bridge? I can't stand how cold that stretch is."

"So, how is the therapy going, anyway?" he asks.

"What do you mean?" she hedges.

"I mean, how's it going? Are you seeing any progress? Any movement?"

"No."

"So, you are not talking about anything?"

Eva stops as they finally reach the other side of the Mass Ave bridge. "Tony, you have repeatedly and specifically told me I can't talk about anything. Of course, I am not talking about anything. I do listen to you."

Tony shakes his head. "You're right, E, I did. I was just testing you."

"OK, see you later."

"Yep."

Tony watches Eva run away. He loves every ounce of Eva: her pure beauty, her strength, her loyalty, her determination, her intellect, and of course her perfect ass. He just wishes, hopes, even prays, that one day, one session, one therapist will actually connect with her enough that she will finally tell her true story. It is painful to watch the woman he loves go through life like a robot, but he understands why she does. When he thinks about what she went through, he can barely tolerate the few details he knows of the story, the story she actually lived through.

LAUREN

Lauren walks into her office at 10:00 a.m. Monday morning, carrying two lattes, one for Maria and one for herself. Lauren has already completed a two-hour workout session and downed an entire pot of coffee at home. Lauren made sure her latte was a skinny, sugar-free, and half-caffeinated.

"Good morning!" Lauren calls out as she walks into her office.

"Good morning!" Maria bounces out of the conference room and into Lauren's office. "Yay, is that for me?"

"Of course." Lauren hands Maria her latte. "So, what does our day look like?" Lauren asks as she hangs up her coat.

"Well," Maria begins slowly as she eyes Lauren's figure. "I would say the day is light, but not nearly as light as you."

"What?"

"You, Lauren, look at you. You are like, just, super skinny."

"Oh, no I am not! It is just the pants; they make me look thin. Trust me, I weigh myself every morning. I am *not* skinny." Lauren retorts.

"Yeah, you are. It is not the pants, Lauren. Your face," Maria hesitates, "you just look really thin in your face."

"Really?" Lauren acts surprised and walks over to the mirror on her office wall. She is a bit shocked at how sunken in her face looks. She knows she is thin; she knows exactly how much she weighs, and it is not much. She needs to get control, because her weight is out of control. She spins back to Maria. "Oh, well, you know I had that stomach flu last week, and I guess I haven't really gotten my appetite back yet. Let's try getting it back today, shall we? How about a big greasy pizza for lunch?"

"You don't have to ask me twice. OK, so you have a gentleman coming in at two o'clock to discuss his daughter's wedding."

"Just the father? Alone?"

"Yes," Marie responds as she hands Lauren a folder with the gentleman's initial client inquiry inside.

Lauren opens up the folder and bursts out laughing. "Are you serious? This is his name, Will Tell? William Tell, seriously!"

"Well, it is actually Dr. Will Tell," Maria corrects Lauren sarcastically.

"Oh, my God. Do you think this is real, or do you think the clowns down the street are trying to spy on our operations again?"

Maria shrugs her shoulders at Lauren's question. "Well, he sounded real on the phone. I guess we will find out. Should I order some apples and arrows with the pizza?" And with that comment, both ladies just start laughing.

BRIOCHE TECHNOLOGIES HOME OFFICE

"John Mack," John barks into his phone as he answers it.

"John, Mark here."

"Mark, good to hear from you. How were your holidays?"

"Good, John; yours?"

"They were lovely. What can I do for you?"

"Well, John, I'm not sure. I got a very strange phone call today regarding someone who works for you."

"Who?" asks John.

"Eva Jackson," says Mark. "Do you know her?"

"Know her? She's one of my best. What was the call about?"

"It was an anonymous caller telling me I needed to look into off shore accounts in her name."

"What? What? Off shore accounts? Mark, what are you talking about?"

"Well, as you can imagine, I was rather confused myself. I pulled some strings, and it looks as though she has a rather hefty account in the Bahamas."

"Mark, I don't know what you are getting at. Eva makes a lot of money; she certainly is one of the top employees. Are you insinuating that she is hiding money from the IRS?"

"I am not insinuating anything, John. I just thought it was odd that I got an anonymous tip about someone who works for you and,

I assume, has some stake in the company that I am investing in. The tip turns out to be true. I don't know why or what it has to do with anything, legal or illegal. But I would like to know, and I wanted to speak with you before I went to the authorities."

"Authorities? Mark, hold on; let's not get ahead of ourselves. Look, Eva has worked for me for a very long time. She is a top-notch performer and person. She is bright, ethical, and makes plenty of money. Let's not jump to any conclusions. Let me look into this. I am sure there is a very reasonable explanation."

"Agreed. I am sorry to give you disturbing news, but as you know, I have a lot of money on this, and the circumstances under which this call came in were a red flag to me."

"Of course, Mark, I understand your concern. However, this could just be a pissed-off employee that Eva had to fire at some point. You are listed publically as an investor, and you are a judge. I am sure there is a reasonable explanation, and I, for one, want to get to the bottom of it, for Eva's sake and yours. I will start looking into this right away and get back to you, Mark. I can't risk any negative press right now with the FDA approval coming in shortly. Will you sit tight until I get back to you?"

"I will. Talk to you soon."

John hangs up the phone and rubs his hands over his eyes. "I need a Scotch."

SESSION 5

The ladies are all rather silent as they walk into Jackie's office and take their usual seats. This ritual always intrigues Jackie. Every time she runs a group, the majority of people take the same seats week after week. *Are we all just creatures of habit, or are we looking for familiarity in an unfamiliar place, or both?*

As Jackie and the others just sit with the silence for a few minutes, Jackie begins, "So, who would like to start?"

The women adjust in their seats, keeping their eyes glued to the floor. Jackie waits; if there is anything she is now very comfortable with, it is silence with these women.

Shelly, never raising her eyes off the floor, begins, "I would like to begin by saying thank you to everyone for last week. I apologize for my breakdown. I needed it. I appreciate how supportive everyone was. I also realize that I did not come completely clean. I just broke down about being a fake. Well…" Shelly takes a deep breath and then, in true Shelly form, just blurts out the rest. "I am thirty-eight, I have been working hard all of my life, and I am in significant debt."

Laruen starts to say something, but Shelly just holds her hand up to Lauren, signifying that she should wait.

"By 'significant debt,' I mean I am in one hundred seventeen thousand dollars' worth of debt, and I do not know what to do. No one knows, except for all of you…well, and the debt collectors, of course. Everyone in my life thinks I should be doing so well, because I am single, and I have worked all of my life. I have a good job, and I make good money." Shelly is on a roll, she still has not raised her eyes from the ground, but she is just going to let it all out. "I have nothing. I own nothing except for some crappy furniture in my five-hundred-square-foot one-bedroom apartment that I rent. I have nothing in my retirement. I am not making ends meet. Sure, I make one hundred thousand dollars a year, but I live in one of the most expensive cities in the country. I have nothing. And I am single, thirty-eight years old, living in a very young, rich city; so to keep up and feel better, I spend money I do not even have. And now I am frigging thirty-eight, with absolutely nothing—actually, scratch that; I have beyond nothing. I do not even have the money to pay for the crap I have. But hey, you want to go out on a date with me? You should know I am worth nothing. You should know I will never have a relationship with you because I will never get close enough to you that I would have to admit my worthlessness. But I will be damned…I will look good, I will fake it, and I will look the part." Shelly stops and continues to stare at the ground.

Everyone sits in the silence for a bit. Eva feels certain parts of Shelly's pain. "I get that Shelly," but before Eva can even finish her sentence, Shelly's rage flares up.

"You get *nothing*, Eva! I am sorry, but really, Miss Four Seasons, 'this is my regular spot; I come here all of the time.' What financial anything do you get? I have had to pay for every penny of my education. I was in debt before I even started my life. MIT, really? Sure, I would have loved to have gone to a good school, but I could not *afford* it. It must be nice to have so many things just handed to you. And seriously, look at you. You could walk around not even showering for days, and men would still throw themselves at you. So what exactly do you 'get,' Eva?"

Everyone is silent, shocked by Shelly's anger.

Eva takes a deep breath. "You really do not know me, Shelly; please don't assume things about me."

"It was…I mean *is* my life." Quietly, Lauren begins to speak. "My life has been easy. Everything has been handed to me, including my education. No, I'm not rich, but I am doing well. My connections, my parents' connections, everything and everyone have made things quite easy. I mean, I work hard. Now my business is completely my responsibility and self-sustaining, but my parents helped; they helped a lot."

Everyone looks at Lauren; her eyes quickly dart back to the floor. They all sit in silence. Shelly is stewing; she is beginning to beat herself up in her head for lashing out at Eva. She wants to apologize but can't. She is still so filled with rage. The rage is consuming her, so much so that she can't do what she knows she needs to: apologize to Eva.

It is taking every ounce of energy Eva has to not walk out the door, giving them all the big middle finger. Here she is, thinking for once she can be real; yet, here it is again. Everyone just assuming they know her, assuming they have figured her out. Assuming she has had everything so very easy. It is her constant catch-22; if she corrects people, then all of the sudden they will feel badly for her; if she doesn't, well…she goes on with her life just as it is. She will go on never trusting anyone and seeing only the worst in people. Or, as per her usual, if she can't speak up for herself, defend, and be honest about herself; she will do it for someone else, or at least deflect the attention.

"Lauren," Eva says, "if everything you said is true, then why are you starving yourself to death?"

Shelly and Lauren are equally shocked by Eva's question as both assumed it would be directed toward Shelly.

"Ah, what do you mean?" stammers Lauren.

"Well, Lauren, I am concerned. I am going to guess that since we have met, you have lost at least twenty pounds that you never needed to lose. If all is picture-perfect, what is the problem?"

Jackie is concerned by Eva's statement. She had planned to address Lauren's weight loss after the session and had already arranged a meeting with an eating disorder specialist. But, as groups so often go, wait for it, and they will put it out there. So Jackie waits.

"I am not sure what you mean, Eva. Yes, I have lost some weight, but I had a stomach bug last week for two days, and it is certainly *not* twenty pounds."

"You are very thin, Lauren," Shelly pipes in; if she cannot get the courage to apologize to Eva, she can at least back her up on what is truly obvious: Lauren needs help.

Lauren looks at Shelly with disdain. How could Shelly possibly betray her after Lauren so obviously stuck her neck out to help Shelly? "Wait, how did this all become about me?" Lauren spits out.

"Lauren," Jackie steps in, "this is not about a focus. This is about what is glaring. You have become remarkably thin in a very short time. How can we help you right now?"

Lauren is now genuinely pissed off, "Well, I will tell you what is not helping: all of you ganging up on me and accusing me of something. I had a friggin' stomach flu; I lost a little weight—sue me!"

"Lauren," Jackie says in her calmest voice, "no one is accusing you of anything. Everyone here seems to be pointing out your weight loss out of concern. Is there something you would like to discuss?"

Lauren gains her composure, thrilled at the chance to regain control. "*No.*"

Jackie just nods her head. The women all sit in silence for quite some time.

"Did something happen to you, Lauren?" Shelly asks in a very quiet voice, her eyes stuck on the floor.

Lauren stares at the ceiling, her hands resting on her forehead. She wishes she could just disappear.

"No." Lauren says, "nothing bad has ever really happened to me. I was chubby in high school and college. Not obese or anything, but I had a good thirty more pounds on me than I should have. My mother made comments a lot when I was growing up. And, of course, my mother was thin and in shape. I think she was ashamed of me. She sent me to a few 'fat camps,' but the weight loss never lasted. After college I started exercising and lost the weight. I was healthy, and people really started to notice me. *Men* started to notice me. I liked the attention and eventually got into a serious relationship. Of course, as the relationship progressed, over the years I started to put the weight back on—five pounds, then ten pounds, and eventually fifteen. My boyfriend would make comments here and there and eventually began to ridicule me constantly about my weight. Ironically, he had a beer gut. We split up after about three years; I found out he was cheating on me. When I confronted him, he basically told me that I should have expected it because I let myself go." Lauren takes a deep breath. "It is not even about my mother or him anymore. It is the constant pressure of being thin, looking good—and now I am forty-two. I did start my own business, and it is very successful. I know I have nothing to complain about. I do not have the debt you have, Shelly, and half the time I feel stupid about what I say. I am lucky and should be so happy. But I am lonely. I hear it constantly from my friends and family: 'Don't you want to settle down and get married?' I hear it from my clients, strangers, everyone. Of course I want to be happy and in a relationship. I own a wedding business, for goodness' sake. I am just so scared. And now, I am scared I am getting old, and I have let go of the dream of having kids. I do not have to let go of the dream of a life partner. I am sick of being alone; I am sick of hearing about being alone; and I am really sick of dating. I spend holidays alone and most nights alone; it is hard. I see so many happy couples all of the time, and I do know half will end up in divorce, but I want that. I want to be a part of that happy couple. I do not want to just settle for the sake of settling, and I am starting to get really scared. I am afraid I am running out of the one thing I do not have any control over. I am running out of time. Have you ever looked in the mirror and not even recognized your own reflection? Have you ever looked in the mirror and just absolutely hated who was staring back at you? Have you ever seen your reflection and thought, *That is the ugliest person I have ever seen?*"

Lauren looks up at the ceiling to try to keep the tears from falling, but it is of no use; they start streaming down her face, and she cries silently, but not alone. The women respect Lauren's need to cry, and they sit with her, hand over the tissues, and give her the time she needs.

As Lauren begins to calm down and wipe her tears, Jackie says, "So you are trying to control the uncontrollable through your weight?" Lauren nods yes.

"Can anyone else in the room relate to what Lauren has been saying?"

Both Eva and Shelly nod their heads yes.

"I am alone most holidays as well, Lauren. It is hard. I applaud you for saying what you said. It takes a lot of courage. Most people think I am cold and unfeeling. I am not. I think I am just afraid that if I break down and let myself feel the loneliness, sadness, and regret, I may not be able to put myself back together." Eva states this with her eyes on Lauren, but her words are meant for Shelly as well.

Eva continues, "It also sounds like you have had some emotionally abusive people in your life—dare I say your mother? That is a hard scar. It is a scar, but one you can't see. It may not do a lot of physical damage, but it sure screws with your head."

Shelly notices Eva's eyes are soft, but without tears and her face stoic. She can't believe what she just heard. She feels even more regretful for being so harsh to Eva. "I am sorry, Eva." Shelly pauses, trying to search for more meaningful words, but she can't find them. "For what I said earlier. I am sorry."

Eva looks at Shelly and gives her a grateful nod. Eva does not blame Shelly for her reaction. Eva is used to that reaction; she has gotten it her entire life.

"And Lauren," Shelly turns to face Lauren, "I can't tell you how many times I have looked in the mirror lately and felt all of those things. And if one more person asks me, 'But don't you want kids?' I think my head will literally pop off my shoulders."

The women all chuckle at Shelly's comic relief.

Wrapping up the session, Jackie checks in with each of the women. All state that although the session has been intense, they are feeling OK. Jackie asks Lauren if she would be willing to see an eating disorder specialist, and Lauren agrees. The women are all very grateful and supportive of Lauren's willingness to work on her eating disorder.

"So I will see you all Saturday morning, nine o'clock, for the make-up session," Jackie reminds everyone. The women all nod their heads in agreement.

EVA

Eva leaves the evening's session quickly, telling everyone she has a conference call with a California company. She quickly walks down Beacon Street toward her home. She is happy that the session was filled with issues from Lauren and Shelly, so she never had to be the focus; however, she is feeling very uncomfortable after Shelly's financial disclosures.

Eva enters her apartment and pulls out her flip phone. She sends a text to Tony: *Her financial situation is very bad!*

Tony promptly responds: *I know. $117,273. I will take care of things. Don't worry.*

Eva: *I can pay it off quickly and anonymously.*

Tony: *I know you can. But let me handle this, E.*

Eva: *OK.*

Eva flips off the phone, leans her head back, and lets out a big sigh. She knows she can trust Tony. She knows he can handle things. She just hates not being in control. Right now, everything feels out of control.

TONY'S OFFICE

Tony puts down his phone and hopes that Eva will listen to him and not do anything stupid. There is a knock at his office door. "Come in."

"Excuse me, sir, do you have a minute?"

"Yeah, Matt, come in. What's up?"

"Well, sir, we have had an interesting development. We got an anonymous phone call today regarding a high-level executive of Brioche Technologies' parent company having a rather padded offshore account."

"Really?" Tony is intrigued by this development

"Yes, sir; we checked into it, and there is a high-level executive with an offshore account that has about three million dollars in it."

"Three million dollars? We're missing fifty million. Who is it?"

"It's Eva, sir."

"What? Are you sure?"

"Yes, sir."

Tony sits back in his chair, shaking his head. "Eva. Something is wrong there."

"Here is a copy of the signature from the back, sir."

Tony stares at the signature. "It's good, but it's not hers. That is not hers. Get a copy of her signature off her passport and have the handwriting expert analyze the two. Check to see when she has been in the Bahamas. I will circle back with Eva."

"Yes, sir."

Matt exits Tony's office and shuts the door behind him. "Bahamas, what the fuck?" Tony says under his breath.

LAUREN

Lauren sits down with Jackie for a bit after the session. She agrees to go to an eating disorder specialist. She knows her weight loss is out of control and is grateful to get more help.

As Lauren walks home, she thinks about everything she said in the session. It is all true. It is exactly how she feels. But there is something more to the problem. The loneliness and the fear are things Lauren has always faced. Yes, she is sad she will not have kids, but she has come to terms with that loss of hope. It is frustrating to constantly be asked the question, "Don't you want kids someday?" The question is so biting, but people with children just do not understand this. They don't know that this question has been asked of her almost daily for years. It grates on her. What is she supposed to say? How is someone who has always wanted children supposed to answer that question? And the arrogance of those who then try and give her solutions like "Have you thought about doing it on your own? You could adopt. How about a donor?" All of it just makes Lauren want to pull her hair out and scream. It is hard enough being alone in the world and trying to run a business, trying to survive; what life could she give a child on her own? The arrogance of these people, who ask these questions and flippantly try and to solutions like it is obvious and easy, makes her insides burn with rage. How do people expect her to answer that question? Do they want the truth? Do they want her to break down in tears and tell them it is the biggest regret of her life? Lauren would love to push her anger out and give these annoying people the flippant answer they deserve to hear: "I do not like kids, never wanted them, never will." How would they react to that? But Lauren knows she could never do that. She is a people-pleaser; instead she just bites her lip, smiles, and responds with the kind, somewhat sad, diplomatic response, "I guess children are just not in the cards for me."

She then has to deal with the constant questions regarding her single status. Yes, she would like to find love; no, she does not know why she has not found it. Yes, she is on dating sites. Yes, she does go out as often as she can. Yes, she knows that someday she will meet Mr. Right. Do they really want to know how lonely it is? Do they really want to know how many nights she cries herself to sleep? Do they want to know that it is, at times, a herculean task for her to get dressed and go out on yet another first date? Do they want to know what it is like to always be the single one in the room? Do they want to know how truly painful it all is for her? They do not. And it is no one's fault. People who ask these questions do not know that she is asked these things day in and day out. They do not know that her life is filled with loneliness and regret. They do not know or understand her pain.

But all of these things are more of a constant for her. These issues are just true in her life and have been for some time. These things are not something that would trigger this weight loss, however. There is some anxiety she feels deep inside herself. She is not sure how or when it got there, but it is different—very different. She doesn't know what it is about. Yet, she has this tight ball in her gut signaling her that something is absolutely wrong. She can't understand this feeling herself; how could she possibly try to address it with the group?

SHELLY

Shelly leaves the session feeling oddly relieved. For the first time in a long time, she is not holding a secret by herself. She knows none of this takes away the enormity of her situation, but admitting it, even to relative strangers, feels really good. She takes her time walking home; even though it is a very cold winter evening, she isn't ready to go home. Yes, she feels relief; however, she knows that at home she has a lot of reality to face, most of it sitting on her kitchen counter, right in the middle of her tiny apartment. No, she is not ready to be alone with that just yet.

Shelly heads down Newbury Street, passing all the shops that she knows she can no longer shop in—shops she knows she never should have shopped in to begin with. She sees all the young college students popping in out of the stores. This makes her angry. Why the hell can they shop here? How can they afford this stuff? This thinking is, of course, what has always led to her troubles. Shelly feels she has just as much right—actually, she feels she has more of a right to shop on Newbury Street than the darn college kids do. She is thirty-eight and has been working steadily all her life. What have they done? Shelly shakes her head and tries to stop her negative thinking, which is what got her into this mess in the first place. Just a few blocks from her house, she decides to head into a little bookshop café and grab some tea.

Shelly is grateful that the bookshop café is relatively quiet for a Wednesday night. She expected more students to be inside the café, studying and jacking themselves up on caffeine. Shelly grabs a small corner table with her hot tea in hand. She sits down with her back to the wall so she can see everyone, but no one will see what she is doing. She sheds her layers and pulls out her laptop. She opens up her Internet search window and types: *How to get out of debt.*

Shelly is amazed at how much information there is on the topic. She suddenly feels less alone as she begins to read stories of how people have gotten themselves out of mountains of debt. The time just ticks away as Shelly becomes more and more enthralled with her reading. She reaches over to grab her tea while keeping her eyes glued to her computer screen, and suddenly, a chill runs down her spine. She keeps her hand firmly on her cup of tea and looks up from her computer. She hadn't realized how much time had passed and how many people have left the café. The chill gives her a creepy feeling. She glances around the room again; everyone remaining looks rather normal. She looks at the time: 9:45 p.m. She is shocked that she has spent two hours completely immersed in her reading about debt reduction. Although she feels less alone in her situation, she is a bit overwhelmed by what steps to take next. The biggest one is making her feel sick to her stomach. It's the one she knows she has to do, but also the one she dreads the most as it makes her feel so very sad. She has to find a less expensive place to live, which means she will have to leave the city. A rush of despair comes over her; she feels as though she could cry at any second. Shelly checks around the room again; she is still feeling pangs of unease amid her sadness. She decides the chill was probably nothing, as she is just very emotional right now. She quickly packs up her things and heads home.

As Shelly walks up to her building she is happy to see that the evening building manager is still at the front desk. She feels a sense of safety after her moment of unease at the bookshop café. He buzzes her in and greets her with a smile.

"Hi, Richard!" she says.

"Shelly," he says, "I have something for you." He fumbles through some papers under the desk and pulls out a large envelope with her name handwritten across the front: Shelly Monahan.

"An older gentleman came by earlier this evening asking for you. He wanted me to give this to you."

"Hmm, that's odd; no one you recognized?"

Richard shook his head no.

"OK, well, thanks, Richard. Have a good night."

"You too, Shelly. See you tomorrow."

Shelly gets in the elevator, and as soon as the door shuts, she shakes the package. It feels like an envelope inside an envelope. Once inside her apartment, she rips open the envelope. She was right; it's another envelope. She opens the second envelope and can't believe her eyes. Shelly places the contents on her counter and feels a wave of panic come over her. She slowly checks her front closet. She then walks into her bedroom and flips on the light. She flings open her closet door; nothing. She heads to the bathroom and pulls open the shower curtain; then she quickly checks under her bed. All clear. She heads back into her living area and does a quick peek under her couch. She heads to her front door and double-bolts it. Even though she lives on the eighth floor, she checks her windows to be sure they are all locked. She can hear her neighbors through her walls, which gives her a sense of relief, knowing they are home.

Shelly looks at the envelope contents on her counter. Still in shock, she slowly makes her way over to the counter and grabs the envelope. She sits down on her floor and spreads out the contents. She counts everything, and then she counts again: $10,000. She rereads the typed note: *I hope this helps. I can certainly help out more. Meet me at Eastern Standard at 6:00 p.m. tomorrow. Bill.*

Shelly is completely confused. "Who the hell is Bill?" she says out loud. It can't be the Bill she dated; he is young. Richard said the man was older. Shelly just sits on her living room floor, staring at what could be very helpful to her, but not understanding any of it. Shelly quickly grabs all of the money piled on the floor in front of her, jumps up, and puts the money and envelopes in a trash bag, which she double-bags and throws in the front closet. She runs over to the sink and scrubs her hands and arms. She frantically vacuums the rug where the money had been spread out; then she washes her countertop and scrubs her hands again. She pours a glass of wine and walks over to the couch. It is too late to call anyone, but she is panicked. She has to tell someone. The police—she will call the police, she thinks. It is all too overwhelming for Shelly; she lies on the couch and just stares blankly at the ceiling.

EVA

At 10:30 p.m. Eva heads out onto her deck to sip some wine and smoke a cigarette. Her head has been spinning since she left the group. She has convinced herself that she is being completely ridiculous. Yes, there are millions of dollars missing from her company. She is not sure why, what, or who, but that is being worked on. She needs to stay calm, not make any waves, and continue to give Tony as much information as possible. Yes, Shelly is in a tremendous amount of debt, but that has nothing to do with Eva. Yes Shelly could be an easy target for a bribe to get to Eva, but no one even knows Eva is in group therapy. No one would ever connect Shelly and Eva. No one even knows that Eva has discovered that money is missing from her company. No one would try to get to Eva through Shelly. Eva is aware that she is being ridiculous and needs to stop being so paranoid. She is living two lives right now, and they are secret from each other. They will stay that way for now, and that is all there is to it. She needs to continue to pretend at work and pretend in group.

Eva takes a long drag of her cigarette and watches the smoke float up into the air. It is frustrating that she can't actually be real in therapy. She wants to be. She actually likes these women. She wants to help Shelly. It is what Eva does—solve problems. She knows just giving Shelly money would not solve anything; but Eva could do more; she could teach Shelly how to handle her money. Money is what Eva knows best. But she can't. She can't get close to these women. She can't use this group the way she had hoped. She hates that she has to lie. It is her life. Her whole life is a lie, based on a lie; she hates it, but it's what she is good at. She has lied to everyone her entire life, and now she has to continue to do so. She can't risk opening up and risk linking any of these women to something they have nothing to do with. She can't risk bringing any trouble into their lives. *There I go again*, Eva thinks to herself. *Justifying my lies like I have all my life. There isn't one person I haven't lied to, not one.*

Eva takes the last drag of her cigarette and then heads inside. She checks her phones and sees that she missed a call from Tony. She then sees his text: *Call me.*

She plops herself down on her couch and calls Tony, hoping he will have some good news.

"Hey, E."

"Hi, any good news?"

"No, no news. Listen, do you have any offshore accounts I don't know about?"

"What?" Eva's tone was a mix of surprise and disgust. "No. Why?"

"I just had to ask, E; we are looking into everything."

"Tony, are you looking into me? I am the one who told you about what was going on."

"No, E. I just need to be sure that I know everything."

"You are lying, Tony," she says. "What is going on?"

"I am not lying, E. I am looking for accounts, and as I do, I want to be sure that I know ahead of time if you have any."

Eva relaxes. Tony's explanation makes sense. He would need to explore accounts everywhere, as it is highly unlikely that if someone were stealing money, he or she would keep it in this country. "No, Tony, I don't have any accounts in any other country."

"OK. Good. Now, why do you keep going to the Bahamas?"

Eva is silent. She feels like the wind has just been knocked out of her. How does he know?

"E?"

"I'm here. You *are* looking into me. What the fuck, Tony?" Eva's voice is bursting with anger.

"E, you have to answer my question. I need to know. This is important. I am trying to help."

Eva continues to be silent. She has been lying to Tony, and she is not sure how to tell him the truth. She clears her throat. "I have a grandmother Tony. She lives there. She is very ill, and…well, she is my only relative. I have been going there to see her and make sure she has everything she needs."

Tony is shocked by what he hears. Eva has never mentioned a grandmother, ever. He knows everything about Eva. "What? Why haven't you told me?"

"I don't know."

"E, this is really important!"

"Tony, I'm not lying. I can prove it. I can show you all of the money I have been sending, and I have pictures. Tony, I'm sorry I never told you. I just…" Eva stops midsentence as she feels tears beginning to form.

"You just what, E?"

Eva begins to cry. "She's all I have left, and she is dying."

Tony's heart aches through the phone as he hears Eva crying. He knows the pain. "E, I'm sorry. I have things to finish here, and then I'll be over. God, E, I'm sorry. I'll be there soon."

Tony waits to be sure Eva is a bit calmer before he hangs up his phone. Eva has a grandmother. The news is shocking to Tony. He leans back in his chair. Eva has a grandmother in the Bahamas. The offshore account is in the Bahamas under Eva's name. Tony had been sure until now that Eva has never lied to him, but she has. *Please do not be lying to me now, E, please.*

SHELLY

The next morning Shelly is woken up by a very painful ache in her neck. She fell asleep on the couch, which is never a good idea after the age of twenty-five. She swings her legs off the couch and rubs her neck. She looks at the clock on her microwave: 5:30 a.m. Then her eyes shift to the closet door. She stands up and walks over to the closet, takes a deep breath, and opens the door. There it is, her double-bagged nightmare, still sitting in the closet. *Shit.* She slams the door shut.

Shelly walks into the kitchen and moves forward with her usual routine: makes the coffee, turns it on, and jumps into the shower. Thirty-five minutes later, Shelly is showered, dressed, and ready to go. She pours herself a cup of coffee and realizes it is only 6:05 a.m. She assumes it is too early to go to the police station. What time does one go to the police station? Where is the police station? Is there a certain one to go to? The thoughts swirling around in Shelly's head are overwhelming. She brings her coffee to the leather chair in her living room and turns on the news. *Oh no,* she thinks. *I hope I never end up on the news.*

By 7:45 a.m. Shelly has run through every possible—mostly bad—scenario that could happen. She has thought about just going to work, not doing anything with the money, and not going to Eastern Standard. She has considered going to the police, but what if she is being watched? Clearly someone is watching her, because "Bill" knows where she lives. Can she just walk up to any cop? The cops are everywhere. Could she just walk up and tell them that she may be being followed? How crazy would she sound? Would they think she was crazy? Would they arrest her? She just wishes she knew a Boston cop or anyone in law enforcement. Right now Shelly is scared to leave her apartment. What if he's out there? What does he want with her? How does he know she needs money? And who the hell is he? Suddenly, Shelly remembers Jim. "Jim, oh, my God, Jim!" she whispers to herself with a bit of relief. Jim is the daytime building manager and a retired Boston police officer. Shelly raises her hands to her face and breathes deeply. How could she have forgotten about Jim? He is her adopted Boston dad. He watches out for her and tells her where she should and should not go (even though she is thirty-eight and has lived in the city for nearly ten years). She goes to him for advice about dating and work; however, most importantly, she trusts Jim.

Shelly jumps out of the chair, throws on a pair of shoes, grabs her keys, and runs out the door. Down the hall she waits for the elevator. The elevator is stopping at every floor but hers, it seems; she pushes the button a few more times, because, yes, everyone knows that the more you push it, the faster it comes. After a few more seconds, which seem like hours, the elevator dings on her floor, loaded with her fellow building mates from the upper floors. She smiles at everyone and squeezes on. It stops a few more times on the way down, but with the elevator car already being so crowded, people thankfully choose to wait for the next one. *On the bright side,* Shelly thinks to herself, *once you move, you will no longer have to deal with this every morning.*

The elevator finally stops on the first floor, Shelly, being close to the door and in the corner, insists on holding the door for the others as they exit. People nod and thank her as they pass. When she looks behind her, there is still one older gentleman remaining in the car; he waves his cane at the open door and says, "After you, Shelly; I insist." Shelly hesitates for a second and then smiles and says, "Thank you, Judge Peterson."

Judge Peterson—how could she forget about Judge Peterson? He can help her; if Jim can't, the judge certainly can. Shelly is amazed at how quickly she has forgotten about the people in her everyday life—the very, very important people, in her everyday life.

Shelly looks over at the front desk. Jim is busy saying good morning to everyone and wishing everyone well as they pass by. Standing next to Jim, behind the desk, is a rather handsome man wearing a jumpsuit of sorts for either a cable company or gas company. Shelly can't quite make out the name from where she is standing, but she is absolutely paying attention to the man wearing the outfit. As Judge Peterson walks by the front desk, Jim's smile gets brighter, as it always does with Judge Peterson; the respect Jim has for him shows all over his face. Judge Peterson was is about to pass by, and he stops to take a second look at the cable/gas guy. The cable/gas guy stands straighter and gives Judge Peterson a quick wink; the judge stands for a second, nods his head, and goes on out the double doors. It happens so quickly, that most would not have seen it. Shelly would not have seen it except she was so taken with the cable/gas guy that she can't take her eyes off him. It is odd; there is some familiarity there. Shelly doesn't understand what just happened, but she knows something just happened.

"Shelly!" Jim calls out, waking Shelly from her trance. Her eyes leave the cable/gas guy, but not soon enough; the cable/gas guy catches her staring at him.

"Baby doll, how are you this morning?" Jim asks, all smiles.

Shelly gives Jim the big grin he deserves. She looks back at the cable/gas guy and sheepishly says, "Hello."

Shelly turns back to Jim. "Jim, when you're done here, shoot me a text. I have a question for you."

"Wait, Shelly, this is my friend Anthony. He is with the gas company and needs to go through all of the units today. Apparently a number of people have been reporting a gas smell in the area. May we start with yours?"

"Um," Shelly hesitates, "well, my place is a bit of a mess right now, Jim."

Anthony waves his hand. "Don't worry, miss; I am not here to judge. I just need to see if there is a leak. It is rather important, and they all have to be done today."

"Um, OK, I guess," Shelly responds, not really sure what to say.

"I am coming up, too, Shelly; don't worry, I won't leave you alone with this handsome man." Jim gives her a wink.

The ride in the elevator feels slow and uncomfortable. Jim and Anthony's eyes are forward, and Shelly just keeps hers to the ground. They exit the elevator on the eighth floor and take a right down the hall toward Shelly's apartment. Shelly looks back before they get to her door, about to apologize again for her mess, but notices that neither of them is looking at her; both have their eyes on the walls and ceilings, as if looking for something. Shelly unlocks her door and verbally apologizes for the mess. Anthony takes two steps in, looks right at Shelly, and asks, "May I?"

"Of course," Shelly responds, gesturing around her tiny abode, signaling it's all his.

Shelly watches intently as Anthony scans her entire apartment. He has some sort of device he waves over everything. She is not exactly sure what waving the device over her couch and table lamps does, but she also doesn't want a gas leak to blow her or the building up. With that in mind, Shelly is OK with him being so thorough.

Anthony walks out of the bedroom, proclaiming, "Everything looks OK in here." He notices the front closet, the only thing he has yet to wave a wand over. He looks at Shelly and asks, "May I?"

Shelly feels her heart beat faster; what can she do? "Of course," she replies.

Anthony opens the closet and takes what seems like forever for a small space; then he shuts it and turns to Jim and Shelly. "Do you have a landline in here?"

"What?" Shelly is confused by his question. "No, a landline, no."

"How about a cell phone?" Anthony asks as he motions to her purse.

Shelly looks at Jim, completely confused. Jim puts his finger to his lips, signaling her to be quiet, and nods at her purse. Shelly opens her purse, her hands shaking, and gives her cell phone to Anthony. Anthony gives her a nod and powers her cell phone off. Now Shelly is gripped by complete fear and holds on to the counter to brace herself for whatever might come next. This is getting too weird for Shelly. Last night some random man dropped off $10,000 for her. Now, her ex-cop building manager and another guy she does not know are alone with her in her apartment after searching the entire place and then turn off her phone. Shelly starts to feel dizzy.

Jim sees the sheer terror in Shelly's eyes and puts his hand on hers. "It's OK, Shelly; he is on your side."

Anthony puts his hand in his side pocket. Shelly sees his hand go into his pocket, and in pure panic, she screams, "Please don't hurt me—please don't shoot me!" She covers her face with her hands.

Anthony quickly pulls his hand out of his pocket. He is holding a wallet in one hand and hold the other up, fully exposed for her to see. "It's OK; I'm not here to hurt you. You are OK. I was just pulling out my ID for you."

Shelly is in a complete state of fear. She feels as though she is in a dream, living someone else's life. She sees Anthony with his hands in the air, a wallet of sorts in one. She looks at Jim, who has a clear expression of concern all over his face.

"It's OK, Shelly." Jim is not touching her but is looking directly at her, "It's OK, baby doll; we are here to help. Let's sit down."

Jim and Anthony help what is now a very frail, shaking, and completely shattered Shelly over to the couch. Anthony helps set her down and then goes over to the kitchen to grab her some water. After a few minutes, Shelly, completely numb, looks up at both men, who have all eyes on her. "What the hell is going on?" she demands. And then before they can answer her, she goes off, "I have done nothing wrong. Yes, I have some debt, but I am paying it. I have done nothing wrong;

what the fuck is happening?" She looks at both men in complete desperation, her eyes wide and filled with tears.

"Shelly," Anthony answers in his calmest voice, "my name is Anthony Mendoza. Most people call me Tony. I am with the Federal Bureau of Investigations. You have done nothing wrong. I am here out of concern. I am here to help you, and I am here to protect you. Shelly," Tony pauses, puts his identification on the coffee table and waits for Shelly's eyes to meet his, "you have done nothing wrong. I want to help you. I am hoping you will help me. I am just here to ask you some questions about something that has absolutely nothing to do with you."

Shelly looks away from Tony, glances at his badge, and her eyes dart back to the floor. She is so scared and confused. How would she even know if the ID badge was real? Her eyes stay glued to the floor. She remembers Judge Peterson; she remembers the nod. They nodded—they knew each other, he knows the judge. Shelly looks up at Jim. Jim sits down next to her and puts his arm around her. "Baby doll, I have known Tony for longer than you can ever imagine. Trust me, you can trust him."

Shelly walks into the Eastern Standard at about 6:05 p.m. She thoughtfully scans the bar and spies an empty seat. She walks toward it, no longer looking around. She does not care who is there. She is solely focused on the prize. Shelly pushes away the sick feeling she has in her gut by repeating her mantra, "It is all about the money." She thinks to herself, "This is your ticket; this is your free pass to start over; focus on the goal." Shelly barely gets herself up on the barstool before she feels a presence behind her—a chill, actually.

"Shelly, glad you came!" Shelly hears a deep, oddly familiar voice coming from behind and to the right of her. Shelly begins to turn to her right, looks down, and sees a cane next to a pair of legs. She now knows the voice, and as she turns toward the voice, she starts to feel faint. "Judge Peterson," Shelly says as she steadies herself on the barstool.

"Hi, Shelly; we are all meeting upstairs in a larger room."

"We?" Shelly asks, completely confused and at this point very scared.

"Yes, the condo association meeting. I assume that is why you are here, for the meeting? I have been elected the designated greeter and herder of cats." Judge Peterson giggles at himself.

Shelly stares at the judge blankly, trying to calm herself down and compose herself.

"Shelly," the judge says, touching her arm, "are you all right? You look awfully pale."

"Oh, yes, Judge Peterson. I am sorry; I may be coming down with something. I, um, I am not an owner. I am a renter. I was, um, just here to meet a friend, but gosh, I, um, am feeling a bit funny right now. I think I will just go home."

"Yes, dear, OK. Do you want me to get you a cab? Or get someone to walk home with you?"

"No, no; thank you, Judge Peterson. I will be OK; it's a quick walk, and I think the fresh air will do me some good."

"OK, then; well, you be careful. Oh look, there is Judy from 503. She looks lost; duty calls. Get some rest, Shelly."

"OK, thanks, Judge Peterson." And with that the judge moves through the crowd, waving to Judy from 503. Shelly quickly gathers up her things and makes a beeline for the door.

Shelly gets outside and clumsily puts on her coat. She turns right and heads up Commonwealth Ave, dodging all of the T riders coming in and out of the Kenmore T stop. A bike rider almost hits her as she darts across Commonwealth Ave and begins to run toward Beacon Street. She feels something buzzing in her purse, but she is not stopping; she just keeps running. She gets to her building, and Richard buzzes her in. Thankfully, Richard is on the phone, so he just gives her a wave as she passes by to the elevator. Once in her apartment, Shelly does a frantic sweep of her closets, bathroom, and under the bed and couch to be sure no one else is there. She double locks her door and is grateful all of the blinds are still closed. She leans on her kitchen counter and puts her head down, finally able to catch her breath. She pulls her smartphone out of her purse; nothing. She then reaches into the zipper pocket of her purse and pulls out her new flip phone. She has four missed calls and one text message reading, *Are u OK? Call me now!*

Shelly takes a deep breath and presses the number 1.

BRIOCHE TECHNOLOGIES HOME OFFICE

"John Mack," John answers his phone in his usual abrupt tone.

"John, it's Katz."

"Katz, where are you calling me from?"

"My hotel room in Chicago. I just left the investor dinner. They are very pleased by the recent publicity about the potential approval."

"Ha, as they should be. Yes, well, marketing at its finest, Katz."

"I don't even want to know what you did to pull that off, John, but nice work. I head back to Boston first thing in the morning. You should know, I am concerned about our Boston boys. I have been seeing them meeting a lot lately."

"Yes, well, Katz, that is what it is, but I think I have managed to get them off our scent for a while."

"How?"

"Let's just say they are concerned about another employee right now, as is the FBI."

"OK." Katz is confused by John's statement, but he has learned to let certain things go.

"Listen, the approval meeting is being bumped up to Thursday," says John.

"Thursday! That is like three weeks early." Katz is shocked by the news.

"I know. So, I guess it is back to Boston and pack up, my friend."

"Yeah, I guess so. See you Thursday."

John hangs up the phone and leans back in his chair. He smiles and thinks, *Poor kid, it's over.*

SATURDAY MORNING MAKEUP SESSION

The women are all very quiet as the time slowly passes them by in silence.

Jackie breaks the silence. "Well, ladies, I would like to begin by checking in with each of you. Wednesday was a very emotionally charged session. Would anyone care to start?"

Shelly keeps her eyes on the floor. She feels as though her body is split in two. One side of her is wrought with angst. She wants to tell the girls all of the things that are going on, the craziness of it all, but she can't. Or more precisely, she promised Tony she would not discuss things with anyone. The other side of her feels so powerful; she sits with the women with whom she finally disclosed her biggest secret, and she wants to be real with them.

"I would like to start." Shelly finally speaks after wrestling through her conflicting emotions. "I would like to begin by first genuinely thanking all of you. I can't express the relief I felt after finally telling the truth. It was the first time, and you are all still the only ones who know. But the relief, it was amazing. I know that my financial position is not any better, but I have started. First by telling all of you I was a fake and then by telling you the exact amount of debt I have." Shelly pauses, inhales deeply, and exhales slowly. She then turns her body toward Eva. "Eva, I want to..." Shelly pauses again, closes her eyes, and shakes her head as she searches for the right words. "I want to tell you how very sorry I am. I had no right to assume anything about you. You have been nothing but kind and supportive to me, and I was a jerk. And using the word 'jerk' is going easy on myself. From the bottom of my heart, I am sorry."

Eva nods her head at Shelly gratefully. "Thank you Shelly, apology accepted. And, honestly, I get it; you are not the first person to assume such things about me."

The two women give each other gracious closed-mouth smiles. Shelly then looks beyond Eva to Lauren. "Lauren, I want to know how you are. Last week was heavy, and you said so many things that I know I can relate to. But I am concerned about your weight, and I hope I am not overstepping my bounds, but I feel a need to say things these days. Well, I guess I always just say things. But I mean I need to say what I am truly thinking and concerned about, not just my typical classic sarcastic comments that usually make someone feel like they have been punched in the gut."

The women all laugh at Shelly calling herself out on her comments. Shelly holds up her hands in surrender to the group. "I know I do it. You are looking a new Shelly, ladies, kinder and gentler, but still real. So truly, Lauren, how are you?"

Lauren smiles at Shelly. She takes a second to gather her thoughts. She actually came to group today prepared to be asked questions and go a little deeper.

"Thanks, Shelly. I'm glad you asked. Last week was hard. The hard part, though, was actually coming to terms with my weight loss. I knew I had lost weight, and I know partly why I lose the weight. I did follow up with Jackie's referral, and I did have a session with that therapist yesterday. Although my weight loss is not under control, I am taking steps. My struggle right now is more…well, it's hard to explain. You, Shelly, had a secret. You were walking around with anxiety and stress because you have a lot of debt. I have had this struggle before, the weight loss struggle. It typically happens when I am feeling very out of control, so I control the one thing I can: my weight. And of course, having been ridiculed before about my weight, it is also like giving everyone the big middle finger. Look at me, I'm thin. Look at how thin I can be. This time, though, I don't know what I am so anxious about. My business is fine, my life is fine, and I am fine."

"Is that part of the issue, everything appears fine and so you are waiting for something to happen?" Eva asks Lauren.

"That's a good question, Eva, and I thought about that. Am I worried about something happening? I was even wondering if I am too fixated on everything being good except for my love life. Is that what this is about? But I don't think it is. I have had this knot in my stomach for a number of weeks now, and I am trying to think back to when it came on. I remember it just coming on out of the blue. I am trying to remember why it came on and when it came on."

"Is there a way we may be able to help you with that, Lauren?" Jackie inquires.

Lauren just shrugs her shoulders.

"Well, did it begin during this group or before?" Eva questions, naturally going straight into problem-solving mode. Eva has, until recently, always been a fan of solving a difficult problem.

"I would have to say it was before group started. Yes, I definitely had the anxiety before group started, but I thought it was just about starting group therapy."

"And you said work is fine and life is fine?" Eva continues with her questions.

"Yes, that is all fine. Really."

"So did something happen over the holidays?" Shelly asks, excited to join in on the investigative questions. "A party, or maybe you saw someone you didn't expect to see?"

Lauren is staring at the floor. She is listening to the questions, thinking, trying to remember. "It wasn't the holidays," she says tentatively as she sorts through events in her mind. "I worked over the holidays, and then there was that snowstorm, so the holidays were actually quite relaxed for me." Lauren sits back and looks up at the ceiling as she goes through the timeline of activities in her head. Lauren sits up quickly as she realizes when everything started. "Oh, my God! Greg Katz! That's it!" Lauren blurts out!

Jackie inhales quickly and feels the blood rush from her face. Lauren sees Jackie's expression and then quickly covers her mouth with both hands.

"What did you just say?" Eva asks, attempting to quell her shock over the words she just heard.

Lauren looks at Eva and then back to Jackie. She slowly pulls her hands away from her mouth. She is overwhelmed with guilt for just having said a name aloud in group—a definite no-no, using a first and last name. "I am so sorry, Jackie! I did not mean to say his name. I'm sorry, I just got so excited that I had figured it out." Lauren looks desperately at the women in the group. "I'm sorry, can we all just erase that name from your minds? I will call him Harry. Harry is the reason I have this anxiety!"

"So does that mean you are Sally?" Shelly asks, trying not to laugh at her own joke.

Lauren begins to laugh. Jackie and Eva are not far behind, but both are using forced laughs as both women are now in shock.

"Sure, I can be Sally. But really, I am sorry. So anyway, I remember. I used to date this guy Harry. We were really doing well and went on trips together; I was falling for him." Lauren pauses as she begins to remember the trip that caused her the most angst.

"What happened?" Shelly asks, dying to know the mystery.

Lauren looks up at Shelly blankly. "Nothing. Nothing happened. Everything happened. But then he just went away, never to be heard from again."

"Bastard!" Shelly pronounces.

Jackie can see the distant look on Lauren's face. There is more to the story. She is trying to think of how to ask questions that would be helpful to Lauren and not further cross a boundary that has already been inadvertently crossed.

"When was this?" Eva asks, back in her problem-solving mode, now with more selfish curiosity.

"Oh, um well, he stopped communicating with me around July. But his name came up recently when I was at a dinner with friends. And that's it. That is when I began to feel this unease."

Shelly leans over almost across Eva's lap and gives Lauren a rub on her knee. "You loved him."

Lauren did love him, but that is not why she feels such angst; there is more to the story, but it's something she can't tell. Lauren gives Shelly an appreciative look. "Yes, I did."

Jackie sits there, trying to stay engaged in her group and wishing she could just disappear and pretend none of this has ever happened. Jackie looks over at Eva, who has become suddenly quiet. "Eva, are you OK?"

"Oh yes," Eva replies, as she sits up straighter in her seat. "Lauren, do you feel better, I mean at least knowing where this feeling started?"

"I do."

Jackie knows that there is more going on with Eva; she also knows that time is running out as far as sessions left, but there is still time in this one. However, for the first time since before she started this group, Jackie can't wait to get the session over with. She has to put away her feelings right now and focus on the matters at hand.

"Jackie, I have a question," Shelly begins. "Prior to us starting this group, you asked us all to write down the answer to two questions. If you had six months to live, what would you do? If you have lived your six months, what do you regret? Why did you ask us that?"

"Great question, Shelly. Any takers?" replies Jackie.

Shelly looks to Eva and Lauren to see if they have any thoughts. The women shake their heads back and forth. Jackie waits another minute to see if the silence will bring forth any great thoughts. It doesn't.

"Well, the questions are often used as vision questions. They are used to get your creative thoughts going and stimulate some thinking around what you truly want out of your life. The first question—what would you do if you only had six months—was aimed at getting to your desires, getting you to think in a grand way. The second had a stronger intent. When you think of what you would regret, sometimes that triggers other things."

"How so?" Shelly asks.

"Well, having told us what you have, what are your regrets?" Jackie asks the question hoping to shift the focus back to Shelly and the group.

"Ha! Where do I start?"

"How about by going deeper than the obvious?" Jackie responds quickly as to not waste any more time.

"Wow. Um, you know that part…the regret part was the fake part of my work that we all ripped up during that first session. I couldn't be honest about my regrets when I couldn't even admit to myself how much debt I had. I regret so many things right now. I guess what I regret the most is allowing myself to…obviously, get this far in debt, but also feel like I had to compete with others by buying things. You know, by being defined by where I live and what designer label I'm wearing. In the moment if made me feel good. It helped me to believe I had 'made it.'" Shelly pauses. The reality of her situation and talking about the feelings behind it makes her feel ill. The regret sits like a huge rock in her stomach, as if she has just devoured a large pizza in five minutes flat. It is a gut-wrenching ache she can't get rid of. She inhales and continues. "I regret that I have sabotaged any relationship I have ever had for fear of someone finding out my truth. I guess I felt like I deserved these things. I was entitled. If everyone else has it, why can't I? I was pretending to be something I wasn't. I wanted to be you, Eva. I was trying to be you."

Jackie quickly jumps in an attempt to not let Shelly project her issues on to Eva. "Let's focus on you right now Shelly."

"I am. I'm sorry. That came out wrong. I meant it. I wanted to be what I see you *as*, Eva. And I mean that in a very positive way. How you look, act, and carry yourself. I don't know what you are struggling with, but from the outside you look really together—and please know I mean that as a true compliment."

Eva gives Shelly the most genuine and empathetic smile Shelly has ever seen from Eva. "I do believe you, Shelly, and I do take that as a compliment. I do."

Shelly feels a sense of relief knowing Eva heard her and believed her. What she said was true and she meant it. "I live in the Back Bay. I live two streets away from Newbury Street. I always see all of these beautiful people, shopping and spending and looking fabulous. I felt like I deserved that too. I wanted to be what I saw around me. I love it when people say how envious they are of me because I live in the Back Bay. People treat me a little differently. People suddenly look at me like I must be successful and smart. I am a fundraiser. I am very good at it. If I were smart, I would be working full-time and doing side jobs at night and on the weekends. That is what I need to do to afford to live here. But I never did that. I kept pretending like I belong here so that I could get that admiring reaction from people. And I would shop when I felt badly—which was all of the time, because I was living a lie. It was a vicious cycle. And I regret everything that I did, because now, I have absolutely nothing. Well, except I have fear. I am afraid I will lose my job. I am afraid of going back to my old habits. I am really afraid of that. And truly, I can't afford to do that."

The women all chuckle at Shelly's last comment. If there was one thing they all appreciated about Shelly it was her sense of humor.

"But don't you feel a little sense of power, Shelly? I mean, it is out there. You have admitted it, owned it. Do you feel any relief? Or is there more you have not told us?" Eva asks this question of Shelly not just for Shelly's sake but for her own as well.

Shelly is taken back by Eva's last question; it's as if Eva can read her mind. There is more. There are some really creepy things happening, but Shelly can't go there. She can't reveal anything about the envelope of money just left at her apartment. Her fear and her interactions with Tony—none of this can be discussed. "No, it is all there. I do feel relief, but I am scared, too. I don't want to fall down again. I can't fall down again. I have so much to do, and there is no net to catch me. I can't afford a net."

Jackie notices the time and realizes there is very little of it left. "Shelly, think of it like moving. You don't just take one big brown box and throw everything into it. Typically you go one room at a time. And even the rooms are broken down into smaller sections—one cupboard or one bookshelf. You are faced with a big task, but you have done two major things. You have been honest, and you have identified a fear. When you look at the whole issue, it can be overwhelming. Let's break it down into very small steps. And that is your homework for Wednesday: starting to break it down and write out the small steps."

Jackie then turns to Eva and Lauren. "You are not off the hook, ladies. Lauren, you may have pinpointed where this anxiety started, but you still are not sure what it's about. I want you to do a little creative exploration. Take a bunch of magazines, glue, scissors, and poster board and sit down when you have a solid two hours of time. Think of Greg—shoot, I mean Harry—and your time together and make a collage of images, words, phrases, anything that stands out to you and symbolizes the emotions you feel. Anything goes." Jackie takes a breath; that assignment was not only hard to give, it will be even harder to work with.

"Eva, I am bringing you back to half of the original assignment. I want you to write about your regrets, right now, as your life is today. I want you to be honest." Jackie then looks at all of the women. "I want all of you to know that it will not be mandatory for you to share your assignments, but I would like you all to do it."

As Eva begins to exit Jackie's office into the waiting room, her phones starts buzzing in her purse. She pulls out her iPhone and sees it is her boss, John, calling. She turns to the ladies apologetically. "Sorry, ladies, my boss. I have to run; see you Wednesday." And Eva runs out the door.

Shelly and Lauren take their time putting on their winter gear. It was a hard session for both of them. Shelly notices a magazine on the table, probably left from one of the other therapist's clients. She takes a second look at the picture and sees something or someone familiar.

Shelly slowly picks up the magazine; it has a large picture on the back cover with a caption underneath reading "Harvard Alumni class of 1968. Judge Mark Peterson, Dr. William Tell, and John Mack."

"Hey," Lauren says as she looks at the picture over Shelly's shoulder. "That's my new client; he is super cool."

"Who is your new client?" asks Shelly.

"Dr. William Tell. I know the name is hysterical, but he is a really nice guy. I am doing his daughter's wedding."

"Huh?" Shelly is stunned.

"She lives in California, his daughter. He is being the dad of the year by doing a lot of the legwork for his daughter. In fact, I am scheduled to meet him in an hour to look at a few venue options. Are you OK, Shelly?"

"Oh." Shelly is struggling with all that she is hearing. "Nothing, I mean yes, I am. I actually—I know Judge Peterson. He lives in my building."

Lauren shrugs her shoulders. "Too funny. It's a small city. Have a good day, Shelly, and stay warm." With that, Lauren heads out the door.

Jackie's office door is still open, and Shelly knocks quietly. "Excuse me, Jackie. Um, this magazine was on the table, and it happens to have a picture of someone I know. Do you mind if I borrow it and bring it back next week?"

"Be my guest," Jackie replies.

Shelly closes up the magazine and realizes that there is a name and address label on the front. "Um, Jackie," she says, holding the magazine out for Jackie, "there is a name and address label on the front cover. I don't want to break anyone's confidentiality."

"Oh, thanks," Jackie replies. "We are usually good about ripping those off. Someone may have left it here." Jackie grabs the magazine and rips out the back section with the label and hands the magazine back over to Shelly. "Have a great weekend, Shelly."

"Thanks, you too," Shelly says with a half-smile as she heads out the door.

Jackie is about to throw away the label when she notices the name: "G. Katz." She looks at the address label and sees what she hoped she would not—Greg's home address. Jackie leans back in her chair, rather perplexed at the oddity of Greg's magazine ending up in her office waiting room.

Shelly stops just outside the office door. She pulls out her flip phone and immediately texts Tony: *I need to speak with you right away.* She gets and immediate text back:

Your place in 30 minutes.

Tony sees an odd text response from Shelly: *No. Judge cannot see you.* It takes Tony a second to figure out whom she is referring to. He struggles to think of where they could meet on a Saturday morning without running into anyone. Shelly's building is certainly not an easy one to sneak in and out of, especially on a Saturday morning.

Shelly reads Tony's text: *25 minutes your place.*

He is crazy, she thinks to herself. She shakes her head, puts her phone in her purse, and heads home.

JACKIE

Jackie spent some time just sitting in her office. She sat and stared blankly at her walls as her mind raced. She replayed everything that had happened in the session. She played with the torn address label in her hand reading "G. Katz." She is confused. She is scared. She is trying to figure out how to deal with this issue in her group. She knows Boston is made up of many small neighborhoods. But really, what are the actual chances that she would be dating a man one of her clients used to date? Jackie has so many questions, and she needs some answers. She texts Rick to see if he and Tom are home and have some time to chat.

Jackie slowly makes her way home. As she walks through the Boston Garden, she takes time to notice the sun reflecting off the snow, making it seem brighter and whiter. It is a cold winter day, but it is Saturday, and the sun is shining. There are many people out and about trying to soak up the winter sun and fresh air, albeit through their multiple layers of clothes. She zig-zags through the shoppers sauntering down Newbury Street. She takes a left onto Dartmouth and makes her way up Dartmouth, crossing over Boylston Street and passing by the Boston Public Library on one side and Copley Square and Trinity Church on the other. Most days she takes in all of these beautiful sights along her walk, but today, she is not noticing much. Her mind is busy playing through different potential scenarios about how things could unfold. Jackie finally makes it to her building. She digs for her keys, pulls off her glove with her mouth, and unlocks the two sets of doors. She makes her way up a flight of stairs to Rick and Tom's apartment. She smiles when she sees their boots outside their door, perfectly lined up on a freshly cleaned throw rug. She sits on the top step, yanks off her boots, and places them neatly next to the others—but not on the clean rug. She can smell something wonderful coming from their apartment, and just as she is about to knock, Rick opens the door.

"I thought I heard someone! Get on in here, gorgeous. You must be freezing; let's get your coat off and snuggle you up with a blanket. Tom is making his fabulous spiced cider." Rick takes a second to sniff the air. "Don't you just love that smell?" He stops for a second breath and looks at Jackie. "What's wrong?"

Jackie tries to gather her thoughts, her head now spinning around Rick's unstoppable energy. "A lot, or maybe nothing. I'm not sure; that's why I needed to speak with you and Tom."

Rick gives Jackie a pouty look. "OK, Tom is just finishing up a call with his mother. He'll be right out. We will have some cider and figure out," Rick pauses, "whatever it is that may or may not need to be figured out."

Tom walks into the living room from the bedroom. "Hi, love. How's our favorite girl?" He walks over and gives Jackie a big hug.

"We may have a bit of an issue here, Tom." Rick says as he points to Jackie from behind her.

Tom pulls Jackie out of his arms, still holding on to her shoulders, "An issue? Is it Greg? What did he do?"

Jackie sighs. "I think we're going to need some cider and a seat; this could be a long one."

Tom runs to the kitchen and gets everyone some hot cider. The trio then sits down on the couch. Jackie can tell the boys are dying to know what is going on. She has to tell the story without giving any names. "Tom, you knew Greg in college and then reconnected with him a couple of years ago, right?"

"Yes, Jackie; we told you the story. I ran into him a few years ago at Flour Bakery, and we just resurrected our friendship. We were good friends in college, so it was easy to rekindle. At first, he was dating someone, and you were with that Neanderthal that none of us liked." Tom rolls his eyes toward Rick, and Rick nods his head in agreement. "Anyway, that's why we did not get you two together until recently."

"Well, how did it all come up? How did that thought even occur to you?"

"Hmmm…" Tom hesitates trying to remember. "You know, Jackie, I think I mentioned you a few years ago. I mean, I thought you two would be great together. I'm trying to remember how it all came up. We have lunch occasionally, and we speak frequently. I have invested a substantial amount of money in the company he works for. It has been a great investment; my stocks just keep going up. Anyway…oh, I remember—that day when you and I grabbed lunch at the place on Charles Street near your office. What was the name of that place? Anyway, you left, and I stayed to grab coffee, and in walked Greg. He actually saw you and asked about you. I said you were single, he said he was single, blah, blah, blah…we all know the rest of that story. So, what has he done?"

"Right, the lunch. I don't know. Maybe nothing. His name came up in group therapy today. He used to date one of my clients. It sounded as though it did not end well."

"Ooohhh," both Rick and Tom say simultaneously.

"That is one thing, and I have to figure out how to deal with that. The other weird thing is that there was an alumni magazine in my office, and it had Greg's name and address on it."

"That is weird. Has he been to your office?" Tom asks.

"No. I mean, he knows where my office is, but he has never been inside."

"Did your client bring it in? The one who dated Greg?" Rick asks intently.

"I don't know. I guess she could have; I didn't look at the date. That is a great point, Rick I mean, maybe it's nothing. Maybe she had it in her stuff and just left it in my waiting room. It sounds as though things ended in July, though. But wait, does either of you think it is weird that he ran into you, Tom, while we were having lunch? I mean, you don't think that was on purpose, do you?"

"No." Tom waves his hand to dismiss Jackie's thought. "He is in pharmaceuticals, and Mass General is right there; he is always in the Beacon Hill area."

"True," Jackie responds, once again reassured by Tom.

"Perfect," Tom says as he claps his hands.

"But what are you going to do about the client formerly dating your current boyfriend?" Rick asks, wanting to get into the more juicy part of Jackie's dilemma.

"I don't know; that one I need to sit with for a bit. I'm not seeing Greg until tomorrow night. I have a little time to adjust to the idea so that I don't act totally weird around him."

LAUREN

After four hours of carting Dr. Tell from venue option to venue option, both he and Lauren are getting quite tired by the time they walk into Lauren's office.

"Lauren, this has been a great day," Dr. Tell begins. "Honestly, my head is spinning, and all of the venues are starting to sound and look the same."

Lauren gives Dr. Tell an empathetic smile. She understands his fatigue; most of her clients experience this a number of times throughout the wedding-planning process. "I know, Dr. Tell; it is a lot to take in, but was there any place that just made you feel at home? Perhaps that reminded you of your daughter?"

Dr. Tell sits back in the chair and ponders Lauren's thoughtful question. "Lauren, that is a great question. I guess I haven't been thinking in those terms." Dr. Tell pauses for a moment. "In all honestly, no, none of those places reminds me of her."

Lauren was taken aback a bit by his response. She had showed him all of the top wedding spots in Boston.

"Look, Lauren, I know I have told you about my daughter and her lifestyle in California. I have told you about her home and her high-powered job. But that's just how she lives right now. She is actually a very thoughtful, down-to-earth young woman. She loves nature, she loves the water, and she loves Boston. Do you have a place that would combine all of those things in one spot?"

Lauren gives him a devilish grin. "I know just the spot, Dr. Tell." She pulls up her calendar on her phone. "Would you have time to take a look at it Tuesday afternoon?"

Dr. Tell fumbles in his pocket and pulls out his phone. "How is three o'clock in the afternoon?"

"Perfect," Lauren replies. "I will confirm with the venue and then confirm that appointment with you by the end of the day."

"Great! And Lauren, we are going to be working together for some time; please, call me Bill."

"Of course." Lauren gives Bill a gracious smile as she stands up to walk him out the door. "Bill, I did forget to ask you, how did you find out about us?"

"Oh," Bill says, all smiles. "Of course, a mutual friend we have. Greg Katz."

"Oh!" Lauren was shocked to hear Greg's name. "Really, Greg Katz. How do you know Greg?"

"I have known Greg for years. I knew him when he was a young, ambitious pharmaceutical rep. And, well, even though he is now a very important vice-president or something, we still stay in touch. We were having lunch, and I told him about my daughter's wedding, and he suggested you. He said you were top-notch. So far, I would have to agree."

With that, Lauren smiles. "Thank you, Dr.—I mean Bill. Greg is a good guy. I will thank him as well. Enjoy your weekend, and I will let you know about Tuesday before the day's end."

Lauren sits down at her desk after saying good-bye to Bill. *Wow, Greg Katz—how many times does he have to come up?* He was certainly someone who had quite an impact on Lauren. She did really enjoy her time with him; but he clearly was not into a relationship with Lauren, or he wouldn't have just disappeared like he did. Well, at least she is getting some business from him. *Maybe that is his way of saying sorry.* Lauren takes a few more moments remembering her fun times with Greg. Then a flash, a mental picture just comes to Lauren: Eva Jackson. All of the anxiety that has been pitted at the bottom of her stomach just seems to spill out into her body. Lauren's hands start to shake. She feels the blood leave her face. She touches her hand to her forehead, and it is cold and wet. She is sweating. Lauren slides her hand off her forehead and over her mouth. She can't move. *Oh my God*, she thinks, *what have I done?*

SHELLY

Tony circles around the back of Shelly's building to be sure the judge's car is not in his designated parking spot. Tony texts Shelly to come and let him in the back door. Shelly is already at the back door, waiting impatiently. They hike up the back stairwell to the eighth floor and slide into Shelly's apartment undetected. Before they do anything, Tony puts his hands to his lips, signaling Shelly to not speak. He does a thorough scan of her apartment as he did the first time he was there.

Tony comes back into the living area and sees an envelope on Shelly's counter with her name on it and a magazine. "Is that envelope what I think it is?"

"I don't know," Shelly responds. "It was handed to me by Ken, the weekend front desk manager, just as I came in. I didn't dare open it. But that's not why I texted you."

Tony does not respond as he opens the envelope. Just as last time, there is another envelope inside with what Tony assumes is another $10,000. The note reads: *For your troubles. Please meet me tomorrow at the same place, 11:00 am brunch. I just have a few questions. Bill.*

Shelly shudders as she sees what is inside the envelope. "Tony," she says as she pushes the magazine over in front of him and points to the picture, "this is why I called you."

Tony picks up the magazine and cannot believe his eyes. "Where did you get this?" he asks as he frantically begins to pull out his phone.

"I saw it on the coffee table at my therapist's office. I recognized Judge Peterson, so I was taking a closer look. A girl in my group looked over my shoulder, and she recognized the other man, Dr. William Tell."

Tony stops and puts his phone on the counter. "What girl?"

"Her name is Lauren, she owns a big wedding planning business in town and she said he is a new client of hers."

Tony has an exasperated look on his face as he picks his phone back up. Shelly grabs his arm.

"There is more. I recognize Dr. William Tell. It took me a second, but I know him. I mean, I've seen him. He bought me a drink one night at the hotel. The time I was with Eva."

"Wait," Tony interrupts Shelly, "did he see Eva?"

"Yes, the night I told you about when Eva 'saved me' from some older guy. That night, Dr. William Tell was the older guy. He couldn't take his eyes off Eva, but that just seems to be the normal reaction of most men around Eva. Anyway, he bought me a drink before Eva came in, and he said his name was Bill. But now I remember, I had seen him weeks before, around Christmas, at a bar on Newbury Street. He nodded at me from across the room, and I remember getting a chill, just a creepy feeling. When I saw this picture, it all came together for me. Do you think he is *that* Bill?" Shelly asks as she points to the money and the note on the table.

Tony picks up the magazine again. "He could be, Shelly; he very well could be. What was here, do you know?" Tony asks, pointing to the ripped-off section of the bottom back cover of the magazine.

"Yeah, it was a mailing label with a name and address. I asked to take this from my therapist's office, so when I saw a name was on it, I gave it to her to protect confidentiality of another client. That's not a big deal, right? I mean, this magazine is all over the Boston."

"Probably not a big deal, Shelly, but this situation has way too many odd links to it. I need that label."

"Well, here, let me get you Jackie's number."

"I've got it." Tony motions to Shelly to put her phone down.

"Of course you do." Shelly rolls her eyes.

Tony takes a deep breath. "Shelly, I need you to sit tight. And by sit tight, I mean you cannot leave your apartment until you hear from me. Under absolutely no circumstances can you leave this apartment, do you understand?"

"Yes, but you're scaring me," she says.

"It's OK. Here is where I can protect you—not that you're in any danger, but just to be certain, I want you to stay here. Do you have enough food and supplies to sit tight for a good twenty-four hours?"

Shelly nods her head yes.

Tony sees the fear in Shelly's eyes. "It will be OK. The man downstairs—Ken, is it? Well, he is suddenly going to come down with a stomach bug. It's going around. I will have my guys fill in. I will also have my guys at every corner of this building. You will be completely safe, Shelly. If you need anything, you text me, and I will get it for you."

"What if there's a fire alarm? It's Saturday, and they happen here."

Tony tilts his head. "Good point." He motions to Shelly to get him a something to write with.

"Kitty," he writes on some scrap paper. "If there is an alarm, someone will come up these stairs," he motions to the direction of the stairwell closest to Shelly's apartment, "calling this word; you go with that person."

"Really?" Shelly scrunches her face, completely confused.

"No, Shelly, not really. If there is a fire alarm, get the hell out!"

Shelly just hangs her head and starts giggling at her own gullibility.

"Look, Shelly, I know this is a tense time. I know I'm asking you to trust me without giving you a lot of information. I will always be one press of a button away. I will have men at every spot in and out of this building. I do need you to follow my instructions right now, but I also need you to maintain your common sense. And your sense of humor! OK?"

"OK." Shelly lets out of sigh of relief.

Tony remains in Shelly's apartment and makes the calls he needs to make to get all of the safety precautions in place. Tony waits to hear from his team that they are in place. He pulls back Shelly's blinds to be certain he can see his team in front of her building.

"Give me your phone," he says.

Shelly begins to hand Tony her iPhone."

"No, the other one."

Shelly hands Tony her flip phone, and he pulls out a new one for her. "Works the same way as the last one. I have to go. Are you all set?"

"Yes, I think so. What about that?" Shelly points to the envelope and cash on the table.

"I will be taking that. Shelly, you are to go nowhere."

"I promise. But wait, Tony, what do you know about Eva?"

"Eva? Why?"

"Well, you know she's in my group, and you seem to know everything about my therapy group. Is this somehow related to her?"

"No. Why do you ask?"

"I don't know. I mean, this all seems too odd, and you had a strong reaction about whether Bill saw Eva that night at the Four Seasons. She seems like she is in a high-powered position that would revolve around money and this kind of craziness."

"Eva is not crazy."

"So you do know her."

"Yes."

"Why is she so cold? I mean, at times you see a glimpse of something, emotion, something, but then she just shuts down. She seems fake, like at first you think she is really connecting with you, but then she shuts down so quickly. It seems like she just knows what to say but doesn't feel anything."

"Do you have emotions, Shelly?" asks Tony. "Do you think you feel things?"

"Seriously, Tony, have we met?"

Tony grins. "We have. Well, most people who feel things would not be able to wrap their heads around what Eva has been through."

Shelly is stunned by the emotion and command in Tony's voice. Thus far he has been her rock, the calm voice, steadying her with his words of emotionless reason. "How well do you know Eva?" she asks.

"She is my best friend—has been since high school. Give me twenty-four hours, Shelly. Do everything I say for twenty-four hours. After that, if you still need to know the story, I will tell you. Can you do that, do exactly as I say for twenty-four hours?"

Shelly nods. "Yes."

"OK, text if you need anything." And with that, Tony slides the envelope and its contents into a bag. He grabs the scrap paper with the word "Kitty" written on it and gives Shelly a wink as he stuffs it in his pocket and walks out the door. Tony doesn't sneak out the back stairwell; he takes the elevator. When he reaches the lobby, he is happy to see one of his men already in place at the front desk. Tony gives him a nod and walks out the front door.

TONY'S OFFICE

Tony storms into his office, absolutely fuming. He passes by his receptionist, who lets him know everyone is in the conference room. Tony pushes open the conference room doors with force, throws the magazine on the table, points to the picture, and says in an eerily calm voice, "How did I not know about this?" Tony takes a seat as his team passes around the magazine.

After some silence, one of his team members admits that he had seen it but did not think it was relevant.

"Not relevant. Not relevant," Tony repeats sarcastically. "I didn't ask for relevance, I asked for all of the information. I now find you irrelevant. Get out!"

Tony's team member just looks at him and begins to try to speak, but he is interrupted by Tony's "*Out!*"

Tony takes a deep breath. He scans the room at the remainder of his team. "OK, we are running out of time. Let's start talking about what we know."

By 6:30 p.m. Tony and his team have made significant progress, but they are still missing a link. Somewhere, they are missing someone. This makes Tony uneasy. He is frustrated by the unknown and concerned about the 11:00 a.m. deadline for the "Brunch with Bill." They need something. They can bring him in, but they need more. They need something to make him talk.

Tony's phone buzzes with a text message. He sees it is from Eva.

Things have changed. Come over. And I think Greg Katz might play a role in this.

Tony looks at the text, puzzled.

Tony flips his phone shut. "I have to go see E. Who is Greg Katz?"

"He is the vice-president of sales for Brioche Technologies, sir."

"Well, get me everything you can possibly find on him. I'll be back. Keep thinking."

EVA

After the phone call with John, Eva went home and took a very long run and an almost equally long shower. She could not believe it. She could not actually grasp what he was saying to her. The whole schedule had been bumped up by three weeks. She had to leave on a plane first thing in the morning to be in California as the government was going to hand down its decision Tuesday morning. Eva absolutely had to be at Brioche Technologies. She has to handle all of the details once the FDA decision is given. Eva knows what the decision is going to be. She knows what the fall out will be as a result the decision. She knows that on Tuesday, people's worlds are going to totally change. They are going to change in a way they could never imagine or expect.

It is seven o'clock in the evening, and it has been dark for a few hours. Eva bundles up in a coat and walks out onto her balcony. It is a very cold but calm night. The water on the Charles is barely moving. There isn't much traffic on Storrow Drive. Eva watches the few cars pass by. She thinks it could be anyone of those people. They could be out having a nice evening in the city, but by Tuesday, it could be over. A random Tuesday, you wake up and kiss your loved ones goodbye. You walk out the door, and you think you are fine, and then you get the news: you have lost everything. Maybe you're retired; you go to meet your usual crew on the golf course, a beautiful sunny day in

Florida, and then you find out that your life savings, everything you have worked so hard for, is gone; you have nothing. Maybe you work at Brioche Technologies; you head to your usual job, the one that has provided you with what you have, the one you have worked so hard at, the one that pays all of your bills. Poof, by the end of the day, it is all gone, up in smoke.

And here stands Eva, out on her balcony, knowing all of this. She does not know any of them. She can't call them; she can't warn them; she can't tell them. She knows that lives are about to be completely destroyed, and she can't do a thing. She thought she had three more weeks to prepare for this. Eva sits back into a chair on her balcony and stares out at nothing.

Tony uses his key to let himself into Eva's apartment. He slowly opens the door and calls for Eva. He walks through the kitchen and into the living room and sees her balcony door open. He slowly steps onto the balcony and sees her. Before he can even say her name, she stands up, her hands covering her face, and falls into him. Tony holds on to her tightly and feels her melt into him. As selfish as it is, Tony loves these moments, these very few moments in their lives when Eva is real and needs him, actually physically and emotionally needs him. But this time even Tony is afraid; he is not sure what this is going to look like, and he can't imagine ever losing the most precious thing in his life.

"E," Tony says softly as he slowly pulls her hands away from her face. Eva looks up at Tony with her big brown eyes. Her eyes are filled with worry and sadness. He brushes the hair from around her face, his thumb gently rubbing her soft cheek. He runs his hand through her hair to the back of her head; he leans forward and presses his lips to her forehead. He can feel her lean into him. He felt the heat rushing through his body. He breathes in deeply, one hand on the back of her head and the other still caressing her cheek. He breathes every bit of her in and whispers, "Let's get you inside."

Tony sits Eva down on the sofa. He gets up and gets her some water and tissues. He sits back down next to her and puts his arms around her. Eva breathes in deeply. This is her favorite spot. This is where she always wants to be; it is where she feels the most safe and the most loved. She wants to bury herself in Tony's strong arms and just stay there. She wishes he had kissed her. She wants him to kiss her. She needs every part of him. She takes a few more minutes and pulls herself up to face Tony.

"I have to go on tomorrow. Everything has been pushed up. The government is giving its decision Tuesday morning. John wants to meet me ahead of time to discuss all of the details."

Tony feels a pang of panic inside of him, but he does not show it. "OK; then we will be ready. Are you ready?"

"No. Yes…I don't know, Tony. I was just thinking about all of the people, all of the innocent people, and the shock and devastation they will feel. One minute they are fine, and the next, nothing—they have nothing."

"Stop," Tony interrupts Eva before she can continue. "E, this is awful, but right now, we have to focus on one thing. Look, you have done nothing wrong; the minute you suspected anything, you called me."

"But Tony, what does that do? I have not stopped anything from happening. These people, their money, it's gone. It's gone, Tony, all of it!"

"You couldn't stop that from happening, E. It already happened. What you are doing is not letting him get away. You are catching the guy for them. That is what you are doing. You are putting everything on the line for them. You are being one of the bravest, most honest, and giving persons I have ever known. Because of what you are doing, he will not be lying on some beach, never to be heard from again. You are giving them the opportunity for justice."

"It's not enough, Tony."

"It never is, E. Now, what about this Greg Katz person?"

"Right, Greg. Well, Lauren blurted out his name in group today. Apparently she dated him and was in love with him, and he just left without any explanation. Now, there is definitely more to this story.

She came up with his name as we were pressing her to pinpoint when her eating disorder was triggered. That's when she blurted out his name."

"Because he left her without explanation?" asks Tony.

"No. They stopped speaking last July, but apparently around the holidays, her friends brought his name up. and she just felt this weird anxiety that she could not pinpoint. But she knows it has to do with Greg."

"That's it? She did not give any other reason? Do you think she was being honest?"

"I do," says Eva. "She is a fairly easy read. I think it has something to do with Katz, but I believe that she is totally unaware of what it is."

"Hmmm. That is odd."

Tony makes sure that Eva is OK for the brief time he will be away. He plans on spending every second he is not in the office with Eva. He makes her promise she will not even pour a glass of wine, let alone go for one of her famously long runs, without getting his approval first. She reluctantly agrees, only because she knows how sensitive things are, and she does not want anything to go wrong.

As Tony is about to walk out the door, Eva just has to ask a question she never asks. "Tony, what were you working on with the whole undercover gay man routine?"

Tony smiles with his hand on the door. "Let's just say I was keeping my eye on a gay judge who is suspected of being involved in a little insider trading!"

JACKIE

Jackie pours herself a cup of tea and curls up on her couch to read. She has thought this situation through and can't think anymore. She needs to free her mind from all of the spinning. If she can relax this evening and get some sleep, perhaps in the morning, she will have a new idea. As she props herself up with throw pillows, her cell phone beeps. She grabs her phone and sees it a text message from Lauren:

I am sorry to bother you, Jackie. I REALLY need to talk to you. Do you have any time?

Jackie puts down her phone and lets out a big sigh. *Apparently, I am not done with the spinning.* Jackie takes a sip of her tea, swings her legs off the couch, and rereads Lauren's text. She could pretend that she was busy, but that would go against every ethical bone in her body. She has to do it. This is not a time to be selfish; this is about a client who has an eating disorder—this is about Lauren. Jackie picks up her phone and calls Lauren.

TONY, SUNDAY MORNING, 8:00 A.M.

Tony is awakened by a text message:
You need to get down here.
Tony rolls off Eva's couch after only having slept for a few hours. He smells coffee in the air and sees Eva out on the balcony, smoking a cigarette. Tony rubs his eyes, stands up, and heads to the kitchen. He pours coffee into the cup that Eva left out for him and then joins her on the balcony.

"You should really quit," he tells her.

"Yes, but I don't see that happening just yet. What time did you get here?"

"About two in the morning."

"Why are you up?" she asks.

"Duty calls, E. I have to go. Did you sleep OK?"

"Yes," Eva replies as she gives Tony a look. He knows how she slept. She knows he checks on her every time he comes in. That, of course, is the reasons she sleeps. Those are her best nights—the ones when she knows he is there.

"I forgot to tell you something last night, Tony. I was so thrown off by all of this being moved up that I forgot to tell you something that happened in group yesterday."

"What's that?"

Eva takes a deep breath and stumps out her cigarette. She motions toward the door for them to go inside. "When Greg Katz came up in group therapy yesterday, Jackie seemed quite shocked to hear his name."

Tony just looks at Eva, perplexed.

"It might be nothing, but she reacted like she knew who he was, or at least his name," continues Eva. "You're not supposed to use first and last names in group. Lauren caught herself right away and apologized. But Jackie's a seasoned therapist, and I'm sure it's not the first time that has happened. Her shock was different."

"OK, I will check out all connections to Katz," Tony says. He hasn't told Eva anything that is going on with Shelly or anything about all of the other weird connections that are popping up everywhere. Eva has enough to worry about. She has one job, and it is the most critical. She has to show up in California and act as though everything is completely normal. She has already submitted her resignation. She just has to see this last part through.

"Oh, my God, Tony, wait." Eva jumps up and runs to her den in a flash of elation. She returns and hands Tony a large envelope.

"What is this?" he asks.

"Hopefully a great deal of help. On the paper is the original list of all of the investors and the projections. On the thumb drive are all of the screenshots of the investors and their actual investments. I didn't want to red flag myself by printing anything out. I assume you have some cool technology that can blow up my screenshots and help with the reconciliation."

Tony is awestruck. "Screenshots. You are fucking brilliant, E."

"Thanks Tony, for everything. And for the record, you could sleep in the guest room, you know."

Tony slips his arms around Eva's shoulders and squeezes her tight. He kisses her forehead. "I know. No running," Tony warns as he gathers his things and heads to the office.

Tony walks into his office and stops short as he sees two women in the conference room talking with one of his team members. His team member stands up as he sees Tony out of the corner of his eye and waves for Tony to come in.

Tony opens the door and introduces himself, extending his hand to each of the women, "Hi. Tony Mendoza."

"Jackie."

"Lauren."

Jackie and Lauren each shake Tony's hand. Tony knows who they are. He sits down slowly and asks, "How can we help you?"

Lauren begins with her story. She tells Tony of her trip to the Bahamas with Greg Katz. She tells him about how they had been drinking on the beach and then they went back to their hotel to shower and change for dinner. She explained that although she had a few drinks, it wasn't enough to black out. But that is exactly what happened. She doesn't remember much after that. It is all just flashes. She remembers waking up the next morning, on the bed dressed in a sundress. She had completely changed out of her bathing suit, but she didn't remember any of it. Greg was next to her and when she told him she didn't remember anything, he said that she changed and then just passed out. They chalked it up to the drinking in the sun. But she was devastated. Lauren had never blacked out before, and it was really unsettling to not remember that much time. When they returned from the Bahamas, that was the last she heard from Greg. She assumed it was because of her blackout behavior. She tried to forget about it, but it was haunting her. She started to have flashes of things—weird flashes. It wasn't until recently that she sort of put things together. She heard Eva's full name a few weeks ago, and then the flashbacks started to get stronger. She remembers signing something but using the name Eva Jackson. She knows she wrote that name on something.

Tony was having a hard time trying to follow all of the details of the story, especially at the speed Lauren was telling it.

Tony just shakes his head, trying to absorb all that he is hearing. He looks over at Jackie. "And why are you here?"

Jackie takes a deep breath, "I am Lauren's therapist, Eva's therapist, and Greg's current girlfriend."

Tony looks up at his team member. "Greg Katz. I guess we have our missing piece."

"Am I going to jail?" Lauren asks frantically, unable to control her angst.

Tony looks at Lauren empathetically, "No, I think we can prevent that. Do me a favor Lauren." Tony hands Lauren a pen and paper. "Sign Eva's name on this paper."

Lauren looks perplexed and does as she is told.

"Tony, I need to give you this, too. I don't know if it means anything but, I found it in my office one morning." Jackie hands Tony the piece of paper with random numbers she found in her office.

Tony looks at the paper. "Do these numbers mean anything to you, Jackie?"

"No. I thought it was from the housekeepers."

Tony gets his team together and makes sure Jackie and Lauren are as comfortable as possible. He sends a text to Shelly, letting her know that he is having someone come to get her and bring her down to his office.

Tony enters another conference room that has all of the blinds pulled. In the middle of the room, three of his team members are sitting around one circular conference table. At the front of the room is a large whiteboard. Written in the center of the board in blue marker is "Brioche Technologies" with a circle around it. Four green spokes are coming from the circle, one reading "Lauren," one reading "Jackie," another "Shelly," and finally "Eva." A red line comes from the blue circle labeled "John Mack." Two other orange lines fall from the bottom of the circle reading "Judge Mark Peterson" and "Dr. William Tell." Each spoke has dotted lines and arrows connecting everyone together. Tony walks up to the whiteboard, picks up a red marker, draws a line coming from the blue circle, and writes "Greg Katz." Tony turns to his team and asks, "Any last thoughts or questions?"

One of Tony's team members point to the board. "How did Dr. Tell know about Shelly?"

Tony turns to the board and then back to the team. "Good question, and I want the correct answer, but we will not be getting that anytime today. I suspect that Dr. Tell was probably following Eva; it is a well-known fact that the company she works for bought Brioche Technologies. Dr. Tell more than likely spotted Shelly coming in and out of the same office as Eva. I am guessing he was just lucky the night he saw Shelly, Lauren, and Eva having drinks together. He probably followed Shelly home that night, and his luck continued, as he discovered she lived in the same building as his good friend Judge Peterson. Dr. Tell and Judge Peterson probably dug up some information about Shelly—easy to do these days—and found a potential weak link to get some information. Both Tell and Peterson have invested a lot of money into Brioche Technologies; they stand to lose everything, and they know it." Tony pauses and looks back at the board.

Another team member speaks up. "Why are Jackie and Lauren here?"

Tony spins around from the board. "I thought you would never ask. That's the best part. Lauren used to date Mr. Katz. Jackie currently dates Mr. Katz. Apparently, this past summer, Mr. Katz got Lauren drunk in the Bahamas and probably slipped a little extra something in her drink. I believe he had her sign some documents to open a bank account under a fake name. What fake name, you ask? I'm glad you did—Eva Jackson. Do we have the signature from that Bahamian bank account?"

One of the team members pulls the document from a folder and slides it across the table to Tony.

Tony looks closely at the signature from the account and the one he just had Lauren write. "I'm not an expert, but I do believe we have a match. Let's get this checked out. This, my friends, brings us back full circle to Christmas Day, when Eva called me to tell me about the fifty million dollars missing from the company. Mr. Katz is not just a Casanova, he is one slippery man."

"Wait, but Tony, how could he get that much money into one account in just four or five months without it being flagged?"

"Another good question. He didn't. I think he has a few million in there, but find out if he has any other accounts. I think Katz has been roped into this as a potential fall guy. As slick as Mr. Katz maybe, there is someone much slicker and much smarter. This money has been flowing out of this company for quite some time. Now, with the doomed miracle drug that is not going to get approved, time is of the essence. Everything is about to blow up in John Mack's face. We need to be sure Mack is caught, and no one gets hurt." As the words come out of Tony's mouth, a chill runs through his body. By "no one," he means Eva.

Tony slides the envelope that Eva gave him to the center of the table. "I need evidence, people. Hard evidence—and I need it fast. Go to it. Oh, and find out what these numbers mean, if anything. Tony places the piece of paper Jackie gave him on top of the envelope." Tony dismisses his team and hopes they find what they need.

Shelly walks into Tony's office and is completely stunned when she sees Jackie and Lauren in the conference room. Tony walks out to greet Shelly. "What's going on?" Shelly asks.

Tony brings Shelly into the conference room and gets her settled with Lauren and Jackie. "Ladies, I am going to need your help," he says. "I am going to tell you a story. It's not going to be easy to listen to. I don't know if it's the right thing to do. I may be hurting Eva by telling you this, or I may be helping her. I don't know. But I do know three things: things are about to change, I need all three of you to keep it together and cooperate with me one hundred fifty percent, and Eva cares deeply for all three of you, more than I have ever seen her care about any other women. Are you ready to hear what I'm about to tell you?"

The three women exchange curious glances and then nod their heads at Tony.

"Good. And then, once I tell you, are you going to do exactly as I tell you?"

"Is that a rhetorical question, Tony?"

Tony winks at Shelly. He has really become quite fond of her.

"Here we go. Eva grew up in a pretty horrible way. Her father was a drug dealer. One night, when she was two or three years old, her father was shot while leaving the house. Right there on their front steps. Now look, Eva didn't grow up in a nice part of town; violence happened all of the time. But to be gunned down on the steps of your home, with your family inside…well, that was harsh even for her neighborhood."

"Did she see it happen?" Jackie asks.

"No, she just remembers the shots and all of the screaming afterward. She did not see her father. After he died, her mother, well, she turned to drugs and alcohol to get through it. She became very abusive to Eva and turned to prostitution to pay the bills. And by bills, I mean paying for her own addiction. There were many nights—almost every night—when Eva's mother would leave her in the car while she went into a bar to get loaded and find a John. This all started when Eva was about four. Her mother would just leave her alone for hours. She didn't care if it was freezing cold or sweltering hot. She didn't care that Eva was only four, alone, and scared to death. When she would eventually return to the car, she was always drunk and drugged out of her mind and never alone. She would put Eva in the front seat and then earn her money in the back." Tony pauses and studies the women's reactions, making sure it is safe to keep going.

"Eva learned to be as still as she could be in the front seat. She learned to make herself invisible. She told me once that she actually believed she was invisible. She said she just kind of trained herself to leave her body so she did not have to hear what was happening in the back seat. But one day, when Eva was about eight or nine, a John reached from the back and grabbed Eva."

"Oh, my God, please tell me she stopped him." Lauren can't stand to hear any other outcome.

"Sort of."

"Sort of! Tony, stop. Just fucking stop." Shelly shoves her chair from the table as she jumps up. She turns her back to the group and rests her head against the wall. Shelly breathes deeply, trying to shake the overwhelming emotions out of herself.

"Shelly, are you OK?" Jackie asks in her calmest therapist voice.

Shelly just stands with her back to the group, her head still resting against the wall, inhaling and exhaling.

After some time, Tony breaks the silence. "Shelly, I know this is a lot to take in. I can stop."

Shelly turns and sits back at the table as abruptly as she left it. "No, I am OK; continue."

Everyone in the room sits silently and just looks at each other.

"Are you sure?" Tony asks tentatively.

"Yes. Sort of, what did you mean by sort of?" Shelly asks.

Tony hesitates for another minute before he continues the story. "Sort of. Addicts are a pretty narcissistic bunch. Eva's mother was very active in her addiction and needed her fix. She told the John he could have Eva, but it would cost him triple the usual fee. I guess the dude got pissed and began slapping the mother around a bit. By pure luck, someone leaving the bar intervened and got the John out of there, and Eva was safe for the moment.

"Eva started to become more aware after that. She grew up quickly. She would leave the car and hide when her mother came back with a John. She even began to drive. Eva never wanted to drive, but her mother would be so out of her mind and would just hit and scream at her until she started driving home.

"One winter when Eva was about ten or eleven, we got a lot of snow. The snowbanks were high, the driving was awful, and the streets were hard to manage for even the most experienced drivers. It was another typical night in Eva's life. Her mom parked the car outside the bar and went inside to do her usual thing. Eva stayed in the car until she saw her mother stumbling out with a John on her side. She snuck out of the car and hid behind a snowbank. Eva came back to the car after she saw the John walk away. Her mother was pretty beat up, and Eva could not wake her. She panicked. She thought her mother was dead. It was after midnight, freezing cold, and no one was in sight. She got into the driver's seat and slowly started to navigate her way to the nearest police car or hospital, whichever came first. She stopped at a red light, and when it turned green, she went. Out of nowhere, a car came and slammed into the passenger side of the car she was driving. That's all Eva remembers of the accident. She just remembers seeing lights shining into the side windows and the sounds of the crashing cars.

"A drunk driver had run a red light and hit her.

"Eva does not remember leaving the car, but she remembers just standing in the intersection, just staring at the damage and not being able to see her mother. The impact of the crash rammed Eva's car into a snowbank. Her mother was lying in the back seat and was thrown out the window over the snowbank. She died. The reports are unclear as to whether she died from the accident, her addiction, or the severe beating she took from her last John. To be honest, I am not sure if that is because of lack of technology or on purpose.

"People who lived on the street heard the impact and called the police and emergency services. They came out to help Eva, but no one witnessed the accident. The drunk driver was killed, and so was his passenger, his eight-year-old daughter, Bailey.

"The first police officer on the scene knew Eva. He knew her mom. He had arrested her mom a number of times, and every time he did, he personally made sure Eva was safe. Occasionally Eva was placed in foster care, but her mother always managed to persuade the courts after a few days in detox that she was on a better path. In those days everyone thought the best place for a kid was with their mother, no matter.

"Eva told the police officer exactly what happened, or as much as she remembered. She knew him; she trusted him. He told her to never speak again unless he was present. He told her that from now on, she was to say that her mother was driving and she was in the backseat, driver's side, seatbelt on. Eva agreed. The officer then went to the car and did something—Eva is not sure what; she just saw him go to the car. He filed his report exactly as he instructed Eva to tell her story. No questions were ever asked. The case was closed. Eva was placed in a group home the next day."

"Why did he lie?" Shelly can't focus on any of the horrific details; she wants to hear something good, anything.

"Well, that was complicated. The drunk driver was known to frequent this less-than-desirable neighborhood, but he was a prominent businessman from a wealthy town nearby. So the officer was protecting Eva. He did not want Eva taking the fall in the courts or the news for something she did not do. No, she should not have been driving, but the obvious fact was the other guy ran a red light and hit her. He killed everyone. Eva didn't kill anyone. But who would believe that? Everyone loved this guy, but they did not know him. They did not know what the cops knew. He had money, and money got him out of everything. Well, everything except this. Eva was not at fault, and this cop knew it. He knew she had suffered more than most. He always said to younger cops that they would see really bad things, really awful things, but the worst things they would see is what people do to innocent, defenseless children."

"Excuse me." Shelly gets up and goes to the bathroom. She braces herself on the walls. The story is too much. It's like hearing a movie but actually knowing the main character. You can't believe it is true or happened. But, it is, it did, and it is Eva's life. Shelly's back slides down the bathroom wall until she is sitting on the floor. *What the fuck!*

After a few minutes, Shelly regains her composure and walks back into the room. "Why didn't he take her in? The cop—why didn't he take her?"

"He had four kids of his own, Shelly," replies Tony. "And on a cop's salary, he did what he could. He watched her. He always made sure she was OK. He made sure she had a roof over her head. He made sure she always had what she needed. He made sure she knew he was always there. He always checked in on her. He still does. To this day, he still checks in—he is retired, but he is still there."

Lauren has been quiet throughout the entire story. She just stares at the wall silently, letting the tears flow down her face. She has so many questions running through her head. Who could do this? Why did this happen? How did Eva survive this? Why was the little girl in the car with her drunk father? Lauren wants to say something but she can't. She is frozen.

Jackie had known Eva's story was probably going to have some bad things in it, but she had no idea just how horrible. She brings her hands to her face and inhales deeply. "So this is why she felt as though she could never completely talk about her fears. She had to put everything in a box in order to move forward. She's..." Jackie pauses as she feels the tears building up inside of her. "What she has done. What she has accomplished, in spite of everything going against her. She's incredible."

"Yes. And you should also know that once a month, she brings flowers to the grave of the eight-year-old girl who was killed—every month for over thirty years now."

"How do you know so much about her, Tony?" Lauren asks, never lifting her eyes from the floor.

"I met Eva in high school. We have been best friends ever since. She may appear be a little broken to some, but she's nothing but pure perfection to me." Tony swallows hard to push down the tears. "Ladies, I am sorry for laying this on you. But again, timing is crucial right now, and I need you to keep it together for a bit longer—for Eva, please."

The women all look at Tony and nod, although confused.

"This is my partner Matt," says Tony. "He is going to take good care of all of you. I need you all to promise you will do exactly as he says."

"Wait! Where are you going Tony?" Shelly asks, panicked that Tony is leaving.

"California," Tony responds as he walks out the door.

EVA

Eva jumps into the cab on Monday morning. It's a usual routine she is all too familiar with, a quick ride to the airport. This particular morning Eva is not feeling so well. She has had her moments along her way of not feeling comfortable about getting on a plane. This time; however, it's different. She is more than uneasy; her chest is actually tight. She wishes she had seen Tony before she left. Eva understands he was tied up at his office; if he could have left, he would have. She knows he is doing everything to help her.

Eva thinks about calling Lauren or Shelly to apologize for having to cancel out on their next session, but she has to brush it off. She feels guilty for just flying off and not finishing what she has started. She feels guilty about a lot of things. Lauren and Shelly will be among a long list of people she will apologize to when she gets home. Eva has to focus on what's in front of her. That's the problem. She is feeling very anxious about everything that is going to happen next. This trip is her absolute last—and her most important.

Eva gets out of the cab when it reaches terminal B at Logan Airport. The terminal doors open as Eva walks through, bag in tow. All of a sudden, Eva stops, and her eyes scan the room. This is a room she knows, a room she is in every single week. Suddenly, she feels like a stranger walking into a small-town bar. She feels as though all eyes are upon her as the room starts to spin. She feels the blood leave her face, and her hands began to perspire as her chest feels tighter and her heart begins to race. Suddenly, Eva feels her body move as fast as possible toward the bathroom.

Her hand shoves through the door as if on autopilot; she drops her suitcase, falls to her knees, and throws up into the toilet. *Oh, my God*, Eva thinks to herself, *did this just happen?* She leans back against the bathroom door and frantically unrolls a large amount of toilet paper to wipe her face and pat the sweat off her forehead. She takes a deep breath and tries to comprehend all that has just unfolded. *Am I sick?* Eva leans against the stall door for another five minutes. *You can do this, Eva. You* have *to do this!*

Eva stands up and unlocks the door. She takes her toothbrush and toothpaste out of her carry-on bag, brushes her teeth, fixes her makeup and hair, and perfectly places everything back in her bag. She leaves the bathroom and heads straight for the security line.

EVA, MONDAY NIGHT

Eva and her boss John exit the dining room and head to the bar. John puts his arm around Eva and squeezes her shoulders. His touch sends shock waves through her body.

"Eva, what am I going to do without you?" he is saying. "I mean, look at you—your last week with this company, and still showing up to help with this process. God, Eva, are you sure you want to leave?"

Eva laughs and smiles at John. He was, at one time, the only man who reasonably resembled a father and mentor in her life. She loved and respected him at one point. Now, just looking at him makes her feel ill; it is all she can do to not explode on him. Eva fondly remembers playing a little game of bullshit with her therapy mates. If there is anytime where she needs to be the expert bullshitter, now is the time.

"John," she replies, "I see it as I have two choices: I leave on top or the bottom. Quite frankly, I prefer the top."

John lets out a larger-than-life laugh, gives her another squeeze, and says, "All right, then. Please, if I can't get you to stay, let me at least buy the woman I've always seen as a daughter a drink."

Eva smiles. "Well then, John, you know I am going to have the best Scotch they have, because I can—and more importantly, because you're buying," she jests while her stomach is in knots.

Eva and John sit and have a glass of the best Scotch the hotel has to offer. Eva is anxious about what to say and how to keep the conversation going. Her disdain for him is seeping through every pore. She knows she can't make one mistake—not one wrong word. She can't let him know that she knows everything. John sips on his Scotch, takes a deep breath, and looks at Eva.

"Eva, you have been more than just an employee to me." Eva tries to interrupt, but John holds up his hand and stops her. He continues, "You have been my mentee, my confidant, and, honestly, the daughter I never had. Eva, we have both made each other a lot of money. However, I have a confession. We have done all of this under false pretenses."

John's face has suddenly changed. He seems pale; his eyes are empty as he looks into hers. Eva has an overwhelming surge of fear come over her. Her heart begins to pound, and her hands begin to shake. She is all too well aware of what John is talking about.

Eva leans toward John, her heart racing. "What do you mean?"

John sips his Scotch and leans forward to meet Eva. He looks into her eyes, drops his head, and takes a deep breath. "Eva, I know everything."

"What are you talking about?" Eva asks in a defensive tone.

"I know you don't have a family in New Hampshire. I know you grew up an orphan and spent most of your life in a group homes. Come on, Eva, you think I didn't do my homework?"

Eva. stunned and speechless, drops her eyes to her Scotch glass, wishing she could suddenly disappear into it. She feels as though she has just been kicked in the gut and had the wind knocked out of her. She knows more than he thinks she does, but she had thought she had him fooled. What an idiot she has been! Of course he knows everything. She knows with whom she is dealing. After a few moments and some long breaths, Eva raises her head and looks over at John and sees that he still has the same cold, blank, empty stare. She is not sure what she's missing. *So what? He knows I do not have a family*, she thinks to herself. *That doesn't mean he knows everything I know.*

"Well, John, that is true. I'm sorry I lied. But I'm not sure why that matters; it was not my family you hired."

"No, Eva, it was not. I hired you because you are incredibly smart and have a remarkable drive to succeed. I did that with a purpose. You see, Eva," John leans in closer to the table, "I chose you because I needed no one to care about you. I needed you to be on the road constantly and not have a family or anyone who cared. I needed to be in your good graces. I needed to become your boss, your mentor, and, well, your one and only. I knew if I did that well, you had to trust everything I did and not question me or question any money that may be missing. You would simply point out errors to me and trust me when I said I would take care of it. Just as you have done."

"What are you talking about?" Eva is completely confused.

"Oh, well, I have taken care of everything. You are forty-three, Eva; you really should know better. I mean, aren't you making enough money? Why would you steal millions from our company and put it in multiple offshore bank accounts?"

"What?" Eva is feeling a tightening in her chest again.

"Apparently, you have been a bad girl, Eva. I understand that you felt so incredibly guilty that you decided to kill yourself. I don't blame you; I mean, how could you live with yourself after ruining all of those lives? Eva, it's in your Scotch. You will have a heart attack in about five minutes. I'm sorry." John leans back in his chair, tilts his head, and watches Eva.

Eva can feel her body reacting to something. She can't believe what she is hearing and seeing. She can't believe any of this. Her heart starts to pound, and her breath quickens. He is trying to pin this on her. This is the ultimate betrayal, that son of a bitch! Eva is so angry and in so much pain. John is just looking at her, just leaning back and watching her. Eva can't even register everything that was just said.

John stands up, his Scotch glass in hand. "Don't fight it, Eva; I'm sorry."

Eva looks at John and says, "This is not over."

At that, John turns and walks away. He walks past the tables in the bar, reaches through the crowd at the bar, places his scotch glass down, and walks out the door.

Eva struggles to stand. She puts both hands on the table and tries to pull herself up but can't. Eva slumps back into the chair as the room starts to spin; her stomach feels like a knife is ripping through it. She starts to sweat even more, and her chest is so tight it feels like someone is grabbing her heart with both hands and squeezing. She leans forward again and places both hands on the table, and with all of her determination, she pulls herself upright and turns to take a step away from the table.

John steps outside of the restaurant and walks away from the entrance. He pulled out a pack of cigarettes, slides one cigarette out, and lights it. He tucks the pack back into his suit pocket and pulls his cell phone out of his other pocket. He has five new voice mails. He stands still, smokes, and listens to his voice mail messages. About three minutes had passed when John heard sirens. *They are fast*, he thought to himself.

He lights another cigarette, not realizing how quickly he is smoking. He pretends to listen to the few voice mails left and watches as first the police car and then the ambulance come to a screeching halt in front of the restaurant. The police officers race into the restaurant. The paramedics jump out of their truck, quickly unlock the back doors, expertly haul out the stretcher, and run it into the restaurant.

John counts to ten. He puts out his cigarette and then calmly and confidently walks into the restaurant. He pushes through the crowd surrounding the table he had left just a few minutes earlier.

"Let me through, goddammit, let me through!" he bellows.

As he reaches the table, he sees the paramedics lifting a lifeless Eva onto the stretcher. "Eva! Eva!" he screams in a panicked voice.

"Sir," a police officer says as he pushes him back. "Sir, do you know this woman?"

"Yes, dammit, what is going on?" John exclaims. "I just went to make a phone call—what the hell is going on?"

The paramedics begin to wheel Eva toward the door.

"Get out of my way!" John tries to push aside the police officer and move toward Eva.

"Sir," the police officer replies, holding him back, "what is your relationship to the victim?"

"Victim? Victim of what? That's Eva; she is my employee! What the hell is going on? I need to go with her!" John yells as he tries to push by the police officer.

A voice from behind John stops him in his tracks. "Officer, we will handle this from here, thank you."

The officer steps away, and John turns to look behind him. As he turns he sees four waiters, one of whom waited on him all night and one who was the bartender. Between the four waiters are two tall men with blue jackets and white lettering reading "FBI." Before John can comprehend what he is looking at, one of the FBI agents asks him to stand with his hands behind his head as another states, "Mr. Mack, you are under arrest for attempted murder, mail fraud, embezzlement, insurance fraud, and money laundering."

"What the hell are you talking about, attempted murder?" John spits, standing with his hands behind his head as an FBI agent pats down his body.

"Mr. Mack, you have a right to remain silent. You have a right to an attorney." John rolls his eyes as the FBI agent finishes reading him his Miranda rights.

"Whatever," John replies. "You have nothing on me, and this is just a big bunch of bullshit for show. God, don't you guys have real criminals to go after? And attempted murder—please, I do not attempt anything! I don't know what you're talking about!"

"Her blood pressure is dropping, what the hell!" The paramedic turns to the FBI agent riding in the ambulance. "I thought you guys were protecting her!"

"We were—*are*! There is no poison in her body!" Tony screams.

"Well, there's something, because this girl is having a heart attack!"

Eva, with an oxygen mask on her face, hears words as if they are being whispered through a tunnel: "Poison…heart attack…protect." She fades in and out.

She faintly hears a man's voice say, "E, stay with us, E; come on, girl, stay with us. Keep your eyes on me. That's it, E." Then all sound fades away into what sounds like a distant tunnel; her eyelids feel like cement, and they shut—but not to darkness, just light.

TUESDAY MORNING

Tony sits next to Eva's hospital bed, just staring and waiting. He has absolutely no interest in the "Breaking News" report that is muffled in the background. He knows all that has happened. He knows they have arrested John Mack for embezzlement, money laundering, and attempted murder, just to name a few. Tony knows they arrested Greg Katz at Logan airport for embezzlement, mail fraud, and money laundering. He hopes they never see the light of day again.

He knows they have even arrested Judge Peterson and Dr. William Tell, along with a few others, for insider trading. At times, Tony feels badly about what Judge Peterson and Dr. Tell got caught up in. They were not trying to harm anyone. They were not trying to harm Shelly or Lauren. They just wanted to get the ladies' assistance in getting their life savings back. They just wanted information they thought Shelly or Lauren might have had due to their connection with Eva. Yet, both Judge Peterson and Dr. Tell knew what they were doing was illegal and wrong. For that, they would pay the consequences.

What makes Tony angry is the reporting, the drama. The news will just keep talking about the people who did everything wrong. They will fail to focus on the amount of pain and suffering these people caused along the way. The news may make a few mentions of the victims who have lost their life savings, of all of the employees who lost their livelihoods, but not to the magnitude of the airtime they give the criminals. They will never give the focus to the ones who most deserve it, the countless victims who have lost everything. And they will not give appropriate mention to the people who were willing to risk a great deal because it was the right thing to do.

Eva struggles to open her eyes, feeling weak and tired. Her mouth is dry, and her throat is on fire. She feels a gentle hand over her forehead. Eva hears her favorite voice. "Hi, E."

She is not sure where she is, but Tony is there. She is OK. She is safe. Still struggling to wake up and speak through what feels like glass in her throat, Eva turns toward Tony, tears beginning to stream down her face.

"Am I broken?" is all she manages to squeak out.

Tony smiles with pure joy and relief to see her awake. He presses his lips to her forehead and continues to stroke her hair.

"I will never spend another second without you. I can't spend a second without you." Tony pauses as he tries to hold back his tears. "No Eva, you are not broken; you are perfect."

EPILOGUE

One Year Later

"Oh my goodness!" Shelly can't believe her eyes as she peeks out behind the stage curtain and sees the thousands of people filtering into the stadium to take their seats. She quickly pulls the curtain shut and turns to the other women.

"There are a lot of people out there!" Shelly's eyes are wide and full of fear.

"Shelly, come on, you can do this. This is what we have been working for!" Lauren rubs Shelly's arm as she tries to calm her friend down.

"I know, but there are so many people! The room is so big!" Shelly replies with a grand arm gesture.

"Ha! Big is what I am going to be in about six more months" Eva says as she rubs her stomach.

"I can't wait for that, Eva. Not that I am wishing you to be fat or anything," Shelly says as she gives Eva a wink.

"Are you going to find out if it is a boy or girl, Eva?" Lauren asks, unable to control her excitement about Eva's pregnancy.

"I would love to know; but my husband suddenly has a desire to be surprised," Eva responds, rolling her eyes.

"Speaking of the devil," Shelly says as she gives the women a nod to look behind them.

Tony and Jackie stroll up toward the women, holding bottles of water and coffees for everyone—decaf for Eva, of course. Within minutes the program moderator comes over to let the women know it is time to take their places onstage. Tony gives Eva a kiss and wishes them all well.

The announcer starts to read the introduction. "I would like to thank you all for coming today to the Grand Opening of Bailey Center for Women. We have four women to thank for all of this, and they are here today. These four women are nothing short of amazing, and this is the grand beginning of something amazing."

The women give each other smiles of support as they feel the energy start to run through their bodies. They will get onstage and give the audience everything they have. Jackie will introduce the women, set the scene, and facilitate the discussion. She will, unlike in therapy, discuss details of her life and the similar struggles she has in common with the other women onstage.

Shelly will discuss her financial failures and how she is making her way out of debt. She will detail the painstaking process of budgeting, having to give things up, and changing her life to live within her means. Shelly will connect her mounds of debt to her feelings of inferiority and let the audience know how powerful she now feels, having control.

Lauren will discuss her wish for love, a wish that was at one point so desperate it almost ruined her life and Eva's. Her desire for love and to be seen as perfect was so out of control that she hid something she knew was wrong.

Eva will reveal her desire for success and what she hid to achieve it. She will stand in her truth. She will stand in her entire truth and not be ashamed of any part of her life. How could she be ashamed? The part of her life that she hid the most gave her the best things in her world—trust and her husband Tony.

The women will connect all of the dots for the audience: how they all lived within blocks of each other, each of them always thinking she was less than, that she was missing something, that she really did not have it all, and that she was the only one feeling this way.

Of course, the drama of being inadvertently and unknowingly involved in a major white-collar crime just adds dimension and drama to their story. But it also brings in more people, and that is what the women want. The proceeds of the event go to their organization that helps women in all areas of their lives. It helps women connect nationally and locally with other women in similar situations and guides them through the process. Whatever women need, their organization helps them: financial guidance, relationship guidance, starting a business, or even just connecting with other people in their own area—anything. Jackie, Shelly, Lauren, and Eva have all combined their expertise to create one organization to help women. The women want others to know that they do not have to go it alone; they do not have to pretend to have it all. The women all know that no matter what we look like, no matter where we live, we are all human; no one is perfect, we are all a little broken, and we all need the support of each other.

QUESTIONS FOR DISCUSSION

1. Was there a character that you could relate to more than others? Who and why?
2. Fear and fear of being vulnerable was discussed as a major roadblock for the women. Has fear ever been a roadblock in your life?
3. Did your feelings about Eva shift at all during the book? How often? When was the shift and what triggered the shift?
4. If you were in Shelly's financial situation and received an anonymous $10,000, what would you have done?
5. Did you ever suspect Eva of being guilty of the embezzlement?
6. Tony and Eva finally came together at the end of the book after a lifelong friendship. Did you want to have that happen? If so, what made you want to see them together?
7. Lauren had an eating disorder. Shelly had a problem with spending. Would you say Shelly had a shopping addiction? Do any other addictions present themselves in the book?
8. What were your feelings about John Mack?
9. Did you think that Greg Katz was falling for Jackie or just using her?
10. Did you ever feel sorry for Judge Peterson or Dr. Bill Tell?
11. Shelly kept the secret about the anonymous money. Eva kept the secret about the crime unfolding at work. Why were they able to keep these secrets? Could you have done the same?
12. At the very beginning of the book, the author presented two questions: If you had only six months to live, what would you do? If you have lived your six months, what would you regret? Did you answer those questions? Were your answers to the questions the same or different?